MRS COUSINS
22/2/14
Mrs Jackson
19/3/14.

KING ARTHUR

KING ARTHUR

J. T. HAAR

Illustrated with line drawings by Rien Poortvliet

LUTTERWORTH PRESS · GUILDFORD AND LONDON

First published in Great Britain 1973

Arthurian legd
CF

ISBN 0 7188 1894 6

Adapted from an original translation by Marian Powell

COPYRIGHT © 1967 VAN DISHOECK, VAN HOLKEMA & WARENDORF N.V.,
BUSSUM-HOLLAND

THIS TRANSLATION COPYRIGHT © 1973 BY LUTTERWORTH PRESS

Printed in Great Britain by
John Sherratt and Son Ltd., Altrincham, Cheshire

Contents

I

Merlin

"Have mercy on me!"

The young murderer's voice rings across Winchester market place, fit to crack the heart. The executioners

have staked him out like an animal. Panic-struck, he circles the post, pulling away as far as his chain allows. Time and again he cries out in terror to the crowd that surrounds him.

Faggots are heaped round the stake. The executioners come forward. In accordance with church law and with common custom, they ask him to forgive them for what they must now do. For a moment the man looks bewildered. Does he realize that his end has come? Dazed, he ducks his head to his executioners. Then he kneels before the cross which a priest holds up in front of him.

"He's praying," murmurs an old woman, and she crosses herself. In a moment the flames will be stretching out for him. How long will he be able to stand the pain?

The executioners take the torches from their holders and thrust the blazing pine-knots into the pyre. The flames begin to lick round the edge of the pile, curling upward through the dry wood. The best killings come when the fire eats slowly through wood and flesh.

"No, no . . . mercy!" He reaches out to God. The chain rattles. The crowded market place is still now, and the terrible sound can be clearly heard in its farthest corner.

"This one comes of tough stock," a peasant mutters. He licks his lips nervously and as if cold, tugs his leather tunic closer round him.

"No, no!" The young murderer twists around the stake. The dense crowd whispers as it watches.

Merlin has pulled his hood down over his eyes. He glances round. Beside him is a serf whose tongue has been cut out in punishment for some offence. He is laughing, and the inhuman sound crackles in his throat. It is the only means of expression left to him.

The people have come from far and wide. A carpenter stands on tiptoe: he doesn't want to miss anything. He sees that the victim is shivering and weeping: bright tears quiver in his beard—the heat of the fire will soon dry them.

The people at the front of the crowd are beginning to give way to emotion. One man murmurs the prayers for the dying: he trembles, realising how fleeting a thing life

8

is. The execution has been carefully staged to make a profound and shocking effect.

Merlin glances at a group of unwashed, unshaven men, dressed in rags and barefoot. They are nudging one another and pointing to the execution fire. They have tramped in to the city from a remote valley; an execution like this one breaks up the grey succession of their days. They are joining in the weeping and the prayers—but they laugh aloud when the boy, frantic with fear, stumbles over his chain.

Merlin looks over the heads of the crowd to the stake. The flames are leaping high now and smoke hides the murderer's face. But his anguished voice cries through the smoke to reach the waiting crowd.

"Hurry!"

But the executioner doesn't hurry. This man must be made an example. Many people are weeping openly. Some are horrified, some stolid: they watch, shivering as they imagine the terror that fills the boy's mind.

There are lords watching; ordinary working men; a holy man; a cluster of women; sluttish girls; dazed children; peasants: they are all touched with sadness as they hear the voice cry out behind the smoke; it is breaking into desperate screams.

Intently Merlin watches: the crowd is deeply moved, yet it finds pleasure in the killing. He shivers. He too is moved, both by the murderer's cries and, still more deeply, by the ignorance of the people who can stand and watch this horror. For an instant he longs to shout his pity. Then he turns abruptly and pushes his way through the throng. A child, holding on to its father's hand, glances up in fear.

Merlin strides away, leaving behind the execution stake and the crowd that is massed around it. He crosses a muddy square scored by deep cart-tracks and littered with muck. Untidily, unevenly, the houses of Winchester lean against each other. Stoneworks, raised by the Romans, are crumbling into ruin. Soldiers guard the gate of the King's stronghold; they are armed with spears, and at their feet lie shields blazoned with gold dragons' heads, though Merlin does not pause to look; deep in thought, he strides on through the gateway. He does not even hear one of the guards greet him courteously.

"Who's that strange fellow?" asks a young bowman.

"Mind your tongue!" the guard says, in alarm. "That's Merlin, the wise man!" He drops his voice to a whisper: "People say he's been given secret powers. He's often called in to advise the King. They say he can see what is to come—that he can bewitch friend and foe alike. Never make fun of Merlin, my lad—you'll pay for it if you do!"

Shaken, the bowman turns to watch the tall hooded man disappear into the King's Hall.

"But who *is* this Merlin?" he asks.

The guard shrugs. "Nobody knows" he says in a low voice. "He lives like a holy man in the wood. He is a—a secret man." In whispers he tells his companion what people say about Merlin.

Merlin stood beside Uther the King on the walls of the stronghold. Here, around Winchester, the dusking hills and fields lay tranquil in the last glow of the sun, but further east, on the borders of Pendragon's kingdom, farms and villages were in constant danger of being raided or burned by the Saxon invaders. Once the Romans had held them back, but now the Legions were gone, the Eagles flown from Britain. And Uther the King could not muster an army to defend his kingdom, for his lords were at ceaseless war among themselves. Their struggles to seize pastures, hunting-rights, fishing-rights, over-shadowed the kingdom. Each lord ruled as undisputed master over his own territory, grasping at every opportunity to increase his power and his acres, and mustering his men to raid the neighbouring lands.

"*That* troubles me more than all else, Merlin," said Uther the King. "I cannot muster an army to throw the Saxons back into the sea."

He stared out across the market place that lay below the walls. The execution was over. The life of the town had slipped back into its usual pattern. Farmers and huntsmen were bargaining over the meat, fish and vegetables they had brought to market. There were the usual beggars, squatting in the muck-heaps around the

church. A few proud lords came riding on horseback through the crowd.

Merlin looked at the King. He knew that Uther, too,

believed him to have secret powers, and he was glad of it, for it was time for him to carry out a plan he had cherished in the solitude of the woods. The people were living in darkness; he must give them a light-bringer. The time was ripe for radical change. Humanity and justice were essentials of life.

"My lord King," he said quietly, "the fate of your people is always in my thoughts. The future of this kingdom is my constant concern." He paused; and what he said then was wonderful beyond belief. "I can promise you victory over the Saxons."

King Uther caught Merlin by the shoulders. "Tell me what I must do!"

"You must give your baby son into my charge."

"*My son*?" The King stared at Merlin, and saw, even in his horror, that it would be useless to ask what lay behind the demand.

"When you are gone, my lord Uther, your son will be High King of Britain. I will raise him up, and he shall be a prince of great renown, a man whose name will shine down the years, world without end. I will help you on this one condition: after your victory over the Saxons you must give your son into my keeping. And you will never see him again."

Uther was shaken to the core. Merlin offered him the safety of his kingdom, but at a terrible price. The decision, thrust upon him, was too difficult for him to make. Helplessly he stared at his counsellor. And Merlin stood there, a man of immense power, a man who knew the secrets of the years to come. The King was trapped.

"I accept your condition. I bind myself to keep my word," the King said in a low voice. "When victory is won, I will give Arthur into your keeping."

"So be it," said Merlin. He placed his hand briefly on the Kings shoulder to seal the contract.

In a clearing in the woods, far from the city and the outlying farms, Merlin paused. Beyond a field, where the corn stood ripening, lay Hector's steading. There was a gate in the stockade and this stood open; through it Merlin saw the courtyard where ducks and geese scrabbled for worms. On a seat against the house-wall sat Hector's wife Iloide with a child in her lap.

A magpie was screaming in the wood. In the bird's voice he heard again the heart-breaking cries of the young murderer. But knowing what he knew, he set aside the memory of that execution and walked slowly towards the farmstead.

Iloide was rocking the baby in her arms, singing softly. For a moment Merlin's sudden appearance startled her, but as soon as she recognised him she smiled and made room for him on the seat beside her.

"Look at my little Kay, Merlin. Isn't he fit to be a King's child?" She held up her son. Merlin touched the baby's head gently.

"Where is Hector?"

"He has ridden out to hunt boar. Our crop was trampled last night," said Iloide.

For a few minutes they spoke of ordinary, everyday matters. From the house came the clunk of the turning spit and the splutter of hot fat in the fire. A friendship had grown up between Merlin, Hector and Iloide. Iloide liked to talk to Merlin. She was comforted by his air of quiet knowledge; and her husband too had been helped by Merlin's insight. Although Merlin had chosen to live the solitary life of a holy man, he liked to talk with this young couple who reminded him of a simple everyday world. He had sought their friendship for a special purpose, but had come to value it for its own sake.

After talking to Iloide for a few minutes, Merlin took his leave. She walked with him to the gateway, her child in her arms, and watched him go, wondering, as she always did, who he was, where he came from, how he had learned all he knew. What had given him his humanity? She had once gone to his hut in the wood, and had crossed the threshold without knocking, to find him staring at a bright sword that lay on the table-board. The blade had flashed in the slanting sunlight. She saw letters engraved on it; she saw that the hilt was stuck with gemstones. Seeing her, Merlin had caught up the sword, and without a word had put it away in a wooden chest. She had never dared to mention the incident. But she was certain that such a sword could belong only to the greatest on this earth.

Was Merlin a king's son? The manuscripts that were crowded on his shelves—Roman scrolls as well as monk-ish manuscripts from beyond seas—must have cost a kingly fortune. Did his knowledge come from book-learning? Sometimes she thought that he knew the ways of other worlds and that his wisdom was the gift of the powers that ruled there. Where had he come from, where did he mean to go? Why did he live in the woods? She had never dared to ask.

Humming softly, Merlin strode along the grassy path. A sense of vocation was strong in him. He was sure and certain. All was ready.

His hut was a small bare place hidden in the leaves. He opened the chest and sprang the secret panel that hid the sword. He drew it out. Then he struck a spark from his flint-and-tinder, kindled three rushlights, and, taking a great pile of blank parchment, he sat down at the table-board.

There was a window high under the thatch. Through this he could glimpse the night sky and the brilliant stars shining tranquilly down on the dark earth. He was thinking of Britain.

Long before, the Celts had left their settlements along the river Danube and travelled westward across Europe to the shores of the northern seas and the great Western Water; some of them had gone on, across the grey water, to land on the coasts of the green rainy island which the Romans, generations later, were to call Britannia. There the Celts had worshipped the powers of earth and sky, and had tried to turn aside the anger of their crowding gods—the gods of wood and tree, river and spring—by killing their own kind. Then the Legions marched into Britain; and through four centuries of Roman rule, the Celtic ways of worship co-existed with worship of the Roman gods. And Christendom had come, like a small living flame—a rush-dip that wavered and sank in a great gale of wind. But the Legions withdrew, and Britain fell again to the barbarians. Her people were once more ruled by fear and force.

As he sat there, Merlin knew that at last a time of change was come. After the long lonely years of uncertainty he saw with absolute clarity what he had to do. The time of preparation was past.

Merlin began to write. At the head of the parchment he set the Evangelist's words:

"*The light shineth in darkness and the darkness comprehended it not.*" He paused, then wrote: *This my book tells of the kindling of a new light in a dark age. In these pages I shall describe the task imposed upon me: the history of the coming of the High King and the gathering of his Knights.*

Today, in the sixth century after the Birth of Christ, Uther the King leads his men against the Saxons. When his victory is won, he will hand over to me Arthur, his son.

Merlin strewed dry sand across the wet ink. He raised his head and stared through his window at a single brilliant star.

2

Arthur's Boyhood

"They're coming!"

Crowds thronged the streets within the city and lined
the Roman Road that led across the open country
beyond the walls. Market-stalls, pedlars, travelling
players—all these were forgotten as the people waited
for the coming of the King and his army. The first
horsemen came riding through the gateway: tired, coated
with dust, stiff with sweat and pride as they acknow-
ledged the cheers.

Behind them came the foot-soldiers. The archers
brandished their bows; "One hell of a fight!" they
shouted. The people stared at the bright hauberks, the

fine shields and helmets, many of which had been split and dented in the battle.

"Look that's the Lord Gorlois." Someone pointed him out. "And over there, in the streaming blue cloak, that's Leodogran, King of Cameliard!"

More horsemen came clattering under the gate-arch: the King's blazon was stitched on their leather tunics.

"The King—!"

The crowd was straining on tiptoe, thrusting, jostling, packed as close as herrings in a barrel. Children were hauled to the safety of their fathers' shoulders. Riding high on his great charger, Uther Pendragon entered his city, the Bishop at his side, to the cheers of his people.

Merlin was standing in the dense crowd close by the gate of the King's stronghold. He saw Uther come riding through the crowd. For a moment their glances met. Merlin smiled. Uther had followed his directions on the placing of his troops and the conduct of the battle; the Saxons had lost the day. The victory would be splendidly celebrated: there would be mock-battles, a feast in the King's Hall, a fair for the people. The inns and the taverns were stacked with casks of beer and mead. The bakers had been busy for days, preparing great heaps of pasties and festival breads. A clamour of church bells rang out over the city.

Under the high roof-tree of the King's Hall, in the smoky light of pine-torches, the lords soon sat at the blackened trestle-tables, shouting and laughing. Servants were scurrying past with great platters of game and poultry, vats of beans cooked in milk, bowls of curds with cream, and huge jugs of foaming beer.

Merlin sat at the King's Board, close to the King. Men were boasting over and over about the bravery of wild Gorlois, and re-telling all his feats of strength against the Saxons; Merlin had closed his ears. As the feasters drank more and more beer, so they grew more boastful, shouting tales and crude jokes, roaring with laughter when one man was drenched by a pitcherful of beer and dragged out by his servant, cheering when another man thumped his fist in a bowl of broth, and again when two others, in a blaze of drunken rage, began quarrelling bitterly—it took a great deal of argument to reconcile the fools. Merlin looked on contemptuously. These were the most powerful men in the land. The mighty Gorlois was dead-drunk now; his head lay on the table in a puddle of grease. There was hardly a sober man left when Merlin signed to the King.

"Merlin, ask me for anything else you choose, but leave me my son!"

Merlin shook his head. He cut the discussion short to spare the King.

"You must keep your pledged word, my lord King," he said quietly. "I too will honour my promise. Your son will be High King of all Britain. He will over-shadow all kings who ruled before his day, and the memory of his reign will over-shadow all kings who rule after he is gone. Bring me the child, my lord."

The King rose. He left the Hall. When he returned, he was carrying his baby son, wrapped in a woollen cloak. "Here is my son!" he whispered. "Teach him, foster him, raise him up as a true king."

In silence Merlin took the child. Gently, carefully, he held the baby in his arms, covering him with a fold of his cloak. He took a last look at the King. Then he turned away and left the Hall.

Carrying the child in his arms, he strode through the city, across the open fields, and into the woods. He walked through the night-hours, reaching Hector's steading at first light on the following morning. There he hid in the bushes and waited, hour after hour, until at last, late that afternoon, he saw Iloide coming out of the gate, with a basket on her arm. Was she going to search for herbs in the forest?

Merlin laid the child on the moss among the ferns.

He took away the King's cloak and the swaddling clothes, and left the baby lying there in nothing but a napkin. For a moment he looked down upon this scrap of humanity. He touched the light hair. Then he drew back to hide behind a mulberry thick-set with leaves.

The baby began to cry. Iloide heard it. She checked; paused; turned towards the whimpering. Merlin saw her bend down, pick up the child, and carry it back to the farm. He heard her calling to her man. For a moment they stood in the gateway, looking round, alarmed and puzzled. Then they went into the house. Slowly Merlin got to his feet. A great cloud spread across the western sky; the last brightness of the sun burned along its rim. It looked, he thought, like Britain herself, cut out in cloud and spread on the sky. He stood motionless, staring at it. Then, without warning, the sun broke through in a dazzle of brightness that lit up earth and air. Was it a sign?

Merlin knew that what he had done was good. As the sun had broken through the cloud, so would Pendragon's small son one day shine across Britain.

With the consent of Hector and Iloide his wife I have undertaken the upbringing of Kay and Arthur. From me they learn horsemanship, weaponry, the customs of the hunt, courtesy, the arts of reading and writing.

I am using all I know to prepare Arthur for the years to come. I am sure that he will be a great king. He is now fourteen years old. He faces life frankly and honestly. He never makes hasty decisions. Kay is wayward and often sullen, but Arthur is a bringer of light.

Iloide crept towards the clearing where Merlin was teaching Arthur and Kay archery. A target had been fixed to a stout wooden tripod. She watched Merlin show the boys how he drew his bow.

Kay tried first: he was hasty and over-eager. As always, he put out all the strength he had; Arthur, however, seemed to know how to husband his strength— he made only half the effort, but the shot was smooth and successful. It was a blessing, Iloide thought, that Merlin had undertaken to tutor them. As he stood there, one hand on his girdle, he hardly looked like a holy man.

"Merlin, show us once more." Arthur's voice was high and clear.

Merlin glanced at the sun and shook his head.

"Go on, once more, Merlin!" Kay's voice was rough and pressing.

Merlin smiled. He picked up his own bow and took an arrow from his quiver. "Very well, once more!"

Surprised, Iloide saw Merlin walk further and further away from the target with the two boys following, until at last, by an old oak-tree, he stopped and turned. Arthur and Kay had told her how strong Merlin was, and how true his aim; she had never given it much thought, but surely a shot from such a range was impossible?

Merlin smiled and said something to the boys. He drew back the bowstring. For a moment the arrow quivered in his grip. He looked at Arthur and Kay and showed them just how he was standing. The arrow shivered into stillness.

Twang!

In astonishment Iloide looked at the target. Quivering from the impact, the arrow stuck fast in the gold.

They were walking back. Now she could hear what Merlin was saying: "It's not enough for your muscles to be strong, for your hands to be steady and your eyes to be sharp. For a really fine shot, you must have more than that."

"You must be—resolute? Certain?" asked Arthur.

Merlin nodded. "Rid yourselves of all doubt," he said seriously. "You must be certain in your heart; certain that you can draw your bow right, certain that you can hit the gold. *That* is what makes your aim sure!"

Iloide stole away. She was grateful for Merlin's efforts on Kay's and Arthur's behalf—surely no other boys in Britain could receive such a schooling—but was it necessary? Why must Merlin implant all his knowledge in them? Was there any point in their being able to decipher ancient manuscripts, living as they did on this remote steading? What plans did Merlin have for them?

Omnem crede diem tibi deluxisse supremum—Slowly, searching for the meaning of the words, Arthur was reading aloud from a manuscript of Horace. Kay looked on without much interest.

"That is enough," Merlin said. He rolled up the scroll and put it on a shelf. Kay looked relieved. The books and the old manuscripts were too difficult for him. He much preferred the lessons in fencing, riding and jousting. But Arthur was as interested in Latin as in archery or throwing the spear.

"Merlin, is there time for a tale?" he asked now.

Merlin smiled. He had been telling the boys tales for many years now: tales about the history of Britain, myths from the shadowy past about Celtic heroes and Celtic gods. In these tales he had stressed, over and over again, that in every tribe, every people, every country, at every time, men had been caught between darkness and light. Arthur and Kay had been fascinated. He had talked to them about the meaning of life. He had shown them that a man must live his life by a pattern, a code.

"A true man should strive to earn the name of knight," he had said one afternoon. Arthur and Kay stared at him in amazement, for this was a word that was new to them.

"What is a knight, sir?"

"A man who lives courageously. His life has purpose. He is merciful. He fights against ignorance. He defends the oppressed."

"Even serfs, even slaves?" asked Arthur. It was a surprising question for a boy of his time: he had grasped the full meaning of the word.

"Even serfs, even slaves. They too are men and they have a right to a life that is worth living."

Time and time again Merlin had talked about the true knight: his code, his courage, his faithfulness. Soon Arthur and Kay became familiar with the word. They even played at "knights" sometimes. A knight was not simply a war-lord; the name meant something more.

Merlin watched the boys. They were sitting next to one another at the table-board. Kay had long ago pushed aside his Latin text. He looked sullen and bored. But with satisfaction Merlin's gaze rested on Arthur. Here his words had taken root.

He spoke to the boys of Christ and His teachings.

"I will tell you another story," he said. And he told them about the bowl into which Christ's blood had drained as He hung on the cross.

"Men call it the holy grail," he said. "The search for the grail is the image of men's searching for the kingdom of heaven."

That day Kay and Arthur went home later and more quietly than usual. Merlin saw them disappear through the wood. Arthur had thrown his arm around Kay's shoulders.

The time was coming near, thought Merlin. In a few more years his task would be completed. Arthur would be High King of all Britain. In a time of war and terror and disease, he would build his kingdom on new footings; a new light would shine in the darkness.

3

The Death of Uther

The prayers for the dying were being said in the King's Chapel. Uther the King, who had stood watchward over his country for so long, was dying. Physicians had been called in, herbalists had tried all the tricks they knew. But it had been no use. The King lay dying, and some of his lords had already come secretly to terms with the Saxons. Across the sea, the Saxons were camped on the shores, weapons to hand, waiting for the signal to storm the island.

At Winchester the King's hearth-companions despaired. Uther still lived, agonized by the dangers that threatened his kingdom, but when he had gone down to death, there would be no one else: no one who could inspire the people to rise in their own defence. True victory seemed far off now, a frail uncertain thing.

Uther Pendragon lay restless on his deathbed. He thought of his son, and of Merlin his counsellor. Where was Merlin now, in this hour of danger?

A servant entered the room.

"My lord King, Merlin asks if he may speak with you."

"Bring him in," said Uther. He raised himself painfully as Merlin came into the King's Room.

Merlin too had grown old. His hair had turned grey, but he was tall and straight as ever, and his dark eyes were still vital and alive. He looked at the King with great affection.

25

"The time has come," he said gently; and the King knew with absolute certainty that his death was at hand.

"I gave you my promise once, I will give it again, and I will make it good. Arthur your son shall sit in the King's Seat after you are gone."

"Tell me about my son," Uther whispered.

"There is no finer boy in all Britain," said Merlin. "He is well-made, he handles his weapons surely and competently, he is generous, he keeps faith. He has wisdom and will-power. He will be a just and merciful man. Rather than rule his people, he will serve them, as a true servant of God!"

As the King listened, the image of his son stood in his thoughts.

"The memory of your son will shine down all the ages of the world."

There was a brief stillness in the King's Room.

Merlin said, "Send for the Bishop, my lord King, and tell him that he may put his trust in me."

Uther the King nodded. Merlin touched his hand. Then he turned and left the King's House.

Word of the King's death plunged the country into blind defeated sorrow. He had left no heir; men immediately began asking who would succeed him. A number of the lords were already claiming the kingship, each trying to gather support. The priests and the people spoke of the King's death with grief and despair; they said that new wars were coming, a battle as great as Armageddon; some said that the end of the world was near.

In despair, a number of lords went to the Bishop. He suggested that they should assemble in the city at Easter. Perhaps, he said, a miracle would show what they should do. He planned to hold a great Easter tournament, believing that this would guarantee the lords' coming, and hoping that they might forget their hatred and envy of one another, and join together peaceably to choose a new king. He sent out messengers to seek Merlin; but no one knew where the holy man had hidden himself. The Bishop prayed to God for help.

Merlin was making his way to the city. He had borrowed a cart from Hector, and with the help of three deaf-and-dumb serfs—chosen because they would be unable to betray him—he had hoisted a great stone into it. In spite of its massive wooden wheels, the cart had almost collapsed under the weight. The horses plodded forward through the dusk, dragging the heavy weight along the old Roman road.

Merlin was thinking of what was to come. He should reach the city tomorrow, and must speak to the Bishop; Hector would follow in a day or two, bringing Kay and Arthur who were longing for the tournament and the chance to measure their strength against the other contestants.

The horses trudged on at a slow clip-clop, led by the serfs, and Merlin's thoughts drifted back to a summer morning, long ago, when Arthur was five years old. He had taken the boy to a quiet clearing in the woods, where lay a great cleft stone—the same stone which was now in the cart. He had shown Arthur the sword, quietly, casually, and had thrust it into the narrow cleft. He had made the boy test it; it was stuck fast, too fast for any living man to pull it free.

And then Merlin had shown Arthur what to do. He must first give the sword a gentle downward thrust to release the secret steel catches that projected from the blade. In this fashion, and this fashion only, could the sword be drawn freely from the stone. Arthur had long since forgotten the morning in the wood, but Merlin believed that when faced with the same problem, he would use the correct thrust. Merlin closed his eyes, walking in a dreamtime; in a few days more the greater part of his mission would be fulfilled.

The city was crowded with people. One after the other, the lords and their men came riding in through the city gates: Lot, King of Orkney, with his lords and his servants following at heel and his banner streaming proudly in the wind; Ulfius, once counsellor to Uther, his bright shield slung round the neck of his warhorse; Baldwin of Brittany riding in to the shrilling of trumpets.

On the clear ground behind the church, tents had been pitched, and here, as the lords looked on, the carts of arms and armour were unloaded. It was clear that the lords were all tense and anxious. Tomorrow the tournament would begin. Tomorrow would God mark out the new king?

Other men came riding in quietly, unaccompanied. Among them was Hector, with the two boys. Arthur gazed round, delighted: the city was crackling with life. Kay, on the other hand, looked sulky and withdrawn, staring at the horses, arms and armour of the mightiest lords in the land. How could he ever defend himself against these men, he in his old-fashioned armour, with his plain sword and wooden shield?

Arthur knew what was going on in Kay's mind and

laughed at him. "Don't be taken in by appearances, Kay. A man who is truly strong doesn't need all this glitter."

They rode to the tournament ground and pitched their weathered tent. Hector went to see old friends, men who had fought at his side long before. Pedlars were strolling among the tents, offering their wares: strings of amber, steel knives, enamelled girdles. Bakers had set up their booths all round the field. The spectators were pressing forward curiously on all sides. Here and there lords were discussing the country's danger. Only a miracle could prevent a long bitter struggle for the kingship. But their gloom did not last long—there was too much to see. Jesters were cracking jokes. Nayntres, King of Garloth, was showing off his dwarf. The brat— a serf's child, born deformed—was chained to his master, who kicked him if he didn't obey orders fast enough.

Arthur and Kay wandered round the city, excited by all the sights. But now it was Arthur who fell silent.

"What's the matter?" asked Kay, surprised.

"I didn't realize—it looks so glorious—but the things that are happening—"

Arthur had watched Nayntres kick the dwarf; a moment later he had seen one of the lords flogging a serf. He stared, appalled, at the faces of lepers. Men, born or made deformed, some with their ears chopped off, were begging for money; the passers-by made fun of them.

"It's the way things are," Kay said.

"Then things must change!" said Arthur; and he thought of Merlin.

"I cannot let you in," said the Bishop's steward. He barred Merlin's way. "The guard should not have let you pass. The greatest men in Britain are waiting to see the Bishop."

Merlin gave him a brief flickering smile. "All the same,

I must see him." He took a step forward and spoke as one who will take no refusal: "Let me pass!"

Startled, the steward stood aside. Merlin passed him, knocked on the door, and entered.

The steward followed him. "My lord Bishop—" he began in apology; but to his amazement the Bishop sprang from his chair to greet the pilgrim with open arms. Bewildered, the steward withdrew. The shabby old man stayed with the Bishop for two full hours—and that at a

time when there was so much to arrange and to settle!
It was unbelievable.

But when Merlin had taken his leave, the steward
realized that the pilgrim's visit had meant a great deal
to his master. The Bishop seemed greatly relieved, as if
a sense of terrible responsibility no longer weighed him
down.

On the vigil of Easter, far into the night, the lords
were engaged in secret discussions. Some hoped that
God would send a sign; but others could not believe in
such a miracle. There was a rumour that Baldwin
meant to seize the kingship and had already enlisted the
support of a number of lords. Nayntres of Garloth, too,
laid claim to be King, and was trying to gather allies. Many
of the lower-ranking lords, knowing that their power
depended on that of the greater men, realized that they
must choose a candidate. They weighed their chances.
A sign from heaven? There was no harm in going to the
Church tomorrow; to pray at the Bishop's bidding. But
they put their real faith in force of arms. They sat around
the campfires talking far into the night. Nobody noticed
the cart which was driven up to the Church, or the quiet
unloading of a great cleft stone.

4

The Sword in the Stone

In the cool sunlight the lords and kings and their men made their way to join the townspeople at early Mass. But as the crowd came in sight of the Church people paused, bewildered, and the endless discussions of candidates for the kingship died away into silence.

In front of the west door of the Church lay an immense stone, and sheathed in the living rock was a bright sword. The hilt shone gold and the gemstones glittered, fit to quicken courage in a man's heart.

The news ran wildfire through the town, and people came running to the square. The Bishop was called to read the runes engraved on the blade. Had God sent them a sign after all?

A great silence spread across the square as the Bishop, fully vested, appeared in the Church doorway. He came slowly down the steps and walked towards the stone. He crossed himself and sank to his knees. The crowd followed his example.

The Bishop rose. He looked around him at the lords and the people. Every man was still as stone.

"God has sent us a sign," he said. "The man who draws this sword from the stone shall be our own true king."

On the word, Baldwin of Brittany sprang forward, clambered up the stone and reached eagerly for the sword. He put out all his strength, tugging until he was breathless; but the sword did not move. He threw off his cloak. His muscles swelled up visibly under the skin. But all his strength was in vain; he could not move the sword. The people crowded in the square murmured a little.

Now Nayntres, King of Garloth, sprang forward, thrust Baldwin aside, gripped the hilt, tugged with all his strength; but the sword was still firm in the stone.

They came up, one after another: the strongest and bravest lords in the land, each with a secret image of himself seated in the King's Chair. They tugged, they jerked, but in the end they were all forced to give up.

"It's a trick of the devil!" Nayntres exclaimed in fury.

"Put a stop to this nonsense!" someone else shouted.

They still came up, one after another. Some knelt briefly, crossed themselves, and prayed for help. Others strode back to their places swearing because they had failed. But the sword was still firm in the stone.

"Bishop, put an end to this!" Baldwin said angrily. "It's bad for the people to see such a display of helplessness."

The Bishop nodded. The people were whispering together: "Witchcraft . . . the devil . . . magic . . ." Troubled, he ordered the marshal to summon the lords to begin the tournament.

As the trumpets cried out, the crowd broke up, streaming away to find good places and arguing about the outcome of the tourneys.

A few soldiers were left in the square, under orders, much against their will, to guard the stone.

Merlin made his way through the crowd to the field where the tournament was to be held. He had stolen Arthur's sword, and Kay's; they swung awkwardly from his belt, hidden by his cloak. He had pulled his hood down over his eyes.

The camp was full of excitement and activity: servants grooming the great chargers, shield-bearers polishing swords and helmets, pages fastening blazoned streamers to their lords' lances. Hardly anyone spoke of the stone in front of the Church. A number of them, including Arthur and Kay, had missed seeing it; they had been too busy with their duties, preparing for the tournament.

Merlin found a place which overlooked the entire field. The Bishop had taken his seat in the great canvas pavilion, accompanied by a number of the lords. The first contestants appeared: the Lord Cambenic, riding on to the field to raise his lance in salute, bow to the Bishop, and turn to canter to his place; and following him on to the field, his opponent, Halech, a younger man but one famous for his courage.

The trumpets shrilled out three times across the field.

Cambenic and Halech spurred forward at full gallop, shields upraised, lances poised: Halech's lance shattered against his opponent's shield in the first lunge, but Cambenic's lance glanced off the younger man's shield and struck him over the heart. He thudded to the ground and lay there; his servants had to carry him away. Cambenic rode triumphantly round the field, cheered by the people.

Kay was seething with anger. In a few moments it would be his turn, his first joust in his first tournament— but his sword had disappeared.

"I'll borrow one for you," Arthur said, trying to calm him; and he crossed to a nearby tent.

"Sir, my brother has lost his sword. In a few minutes he will be called into the lists. Would you lend him a sword?"

"Sorry, my young friend." The man grinned. "There are two things I don't lend to anyone. One is my sword, the other is my wife." His servant roared with laughter.

Arthur apologized and went on. He tried one tent after another, but no one was willing to lend him a sword. At last he paused at the far end of the field, not far from the Church. And it was then that he saw the great stone lying by the Church door, and the bright sword sheathed in the rock.

Without stopping to think he ran towards it. The place was deserted, not a soul to be seen. The guards had slipped away to watch the tournament: after all, they reasoned, the sword was stuck fast in a rock the size of a house; what harm could come to it?

Arthur sprang up the stone. For a moment his hand rested on the hilt of the sword. Guided by a long-ago memory, he pressed the blade downwards. Then, lightly and easily, he drew the sword from the stone. It lay shining in his hands.

The Bishop's steward, watching from his window, caught his breath. A young man was standing on the stone. And the sword itself lay in his hands.

Shaken, the steward made the sign of the cross. This boy, in his plain tunic and sandals—could such a boy be their chosen king? It was unthinkable. He shouted for a servant and sent him off with a message to the Bishop,

then ran out into the square. But the young man with the sword had disappeared.

Arthur went racing back to the field as fast as he could. He thrust the sword into Kay's hand.

"Where did you get this?"

"There's no time to tell you now," said Arthur. He untied the horse and led it forward. "It's a sword fit for a king, Kay. With such a sword you're sure to win!" He helped Kay to mount and followed him to the lists.

Just as Kay was about to ride forward and bow, someone came running across the field in great excitement, and made straight for the Bishop. There was a hurried exchange. The Bishop rose from his seat. He raised his arms to command silence. The clamour of voices ceased.

"Lords and people, the sword has gone from the stone!"

Kay looked round. He heard the trumpets shrill out to signal a pause. He saw Arthur staring at the pavilion in dismay.

"What's the matter?" he called.

"Don't you know?" said a man who, like Kay, was waiting to ride into the lists. "There was a rock in front of the Church, a huge thing, and a sword stuck in it, a real treasure that—" He broke off suddenly. He stared at Kay. "Devil take us—Where did you get that sword?"

"From my brother," Kay muttered, embarrassed. Did the man think he had stolen it?

"Where is your brother?"

Kay pointed out Arthur. People were pressing round on all sides. Someone seized his horse's rein, and he saw two lords grip Arthur by his arms. They thrust him towards the pavilion. The crowd surged forward. It seemed as incoherent as a dream.

They found themselves standing in front of the pavilion. The Bishop bent forward. "Where did you find that sword?" Kay was too confused to answer; he pointed to Arthur.

"Did you indeed draw this sword from the stone?"

The Bishop asked the same question three times, and each time Arthur gave the same reply.

"Yes, my lord Bishop. My brother needed a sword and this one was standing unguarded in the stone."

They asked him who he was and where he had come from. Then the Bishop came down from the pavilion. He led Arthur to where the stone lay in front of the Church. The people came crowding after them, forgetting the tournament. How could this fair-headed boy have done what the strongest men had failed to do?

The Bishop turned to the crowd. "For the sake of the country, I beg the lords to accept the sign God has sent us." Then he thrust the sword into the cleft once more, and called for the strongest and mightiest lords to try their strength again.

Baldwin came forward, followed by Mark, King of Cornwall, the mighty Pellinore, Ulfius, Lot of Orkney, Nayntres of Garloth. They put out all the strength they had; but the sword was sheathed firmly in the stone.

The Bishop nodded to Arthur. He led him up to the stone. The boy stood there, his hair lifting on the wind. His eyes were tranquil. He stood like a king. The people watched, still as stone.

For a moment Arthur glanced round in surprise. He looked out over the people, over the lords. Baldwin was staring sourly ahead. Nayntres the King looked furious. But one of the younger lords gave him an encouraging flick of salute.

Arthur gripped the hilt. For a moment he let the weight of his arm rest on it. Unconsciously he pressed downward: then, without any visible effort, he drew the sword from the stone and lifted it high above his head.

The people, so quick to forget miracles, and yet so anxious to believe in them, began to cheer.

"Long live the King! Long live the King!"

Many of the younger lords swung up their swords to brandish them high overhead. Briefly the threatened struggle seemed forgotten. And forgotten too were the Saxons, poised ready to invade.

The people did not notice Nayntres stride away, most of his chieftains following him. In their excitement they did not see Baldwin of Brittany gather his supporters around him and withdraw to his camp. They did not see, or want to see, that many of the great lords looked at the boy with hatred or mistrust.

Merlin hurried to the lords' camp, to see and hear what he could. With increasing anxiety he caught snatches of conversation.

"What use is a brat like that?" one lord was saying in his tent. "I owe him nothing, and I'll take no oath to be his man."

A few yards further on Merlin heard Baldwin of Brittany saying, "That boy Arthur has grown up in the wilds like any peasant's son. Are we to see a farmboy in the King's Seat? Is a peasant to lead us against the Saxons?"

Anger burned up in Merlin. He had expected some of the lords to react in this way; but he was shaken to see that others too, men like Pellinore and Leodogran, were listening without protest.

He paused again by Cambenic's scarlet tent. Here too he heard men belittling Arthur behind his back. For a moment Merlin lost his self-control. He broke the ranks of Cambenic's men, and said bitingly:

"Bragging cannot hurt Arthur the King, it only makes you look a fool."

Cambenic drew his sword.

"I'll teach you proper manners—"

Merlin seized him by the wrist. The lords held their breath. What was this fool pilgrim doing? Didn't he realize that Cambenic was killing-mad?

But as they watched, the pilgrim no longer looked such a foolish old man. Flushed with anger, Cambenic strained to break the grip on his arm, but the pilgrim held him fast, then caught hold of the other wrist also. He made no visible effort, yet Cambenic could not break free. The watchers murmured among themselves. Cambenic's sword clattered to the ground. The pilgrim was bending Cambenic over in a great arc: his grip must be strong as iron. The lords watched in amazement.

Ashamed of his loss of self-control, Merlin jerked his opponent upright, released him and, without once looking round, walked away. Behind him Cambenic burst into furious shouting. Fortunately his friends managed to quieten him.

The Bishop looked at his young king. He was smiling, but his eyes were troubled.

"My lord King," he said; and paused. It was the first time Arthur had been called by the King's name. "The oath you mean to take is a fine one, but many of the lords will object to the wording."

"I cannot change the wording in any way."

The Bishop rose and walked to the window. The oath Arthur wanted to make might impress some of the younger lords, but their support was not enough; it would not help him to establish the kingdom in peace. Men were saying that Nayntres and Baldwin had formed an alliance. They were already talking of a plot against the King.

Yet although Arthur was young, he seemed to know exactly what he meant to do—

"So be it," the Bishop said.

"Why did you want me to change the wording of my oath?"

"Because it will bring trouble. I am afraid you will find yourself standing alone among enemies as a stag is bayed by hounds. Ideals will not help you there. You are very young, my lord King."

"We are not here to speak of my youth," said Arthur. "I have been called to the kingship. It may cost me everything I have, but I cannot turn back from the King's Seat."

The Bishop bowed his head. "So be it, my lord, Arthur the King."

5

The Crowning of the King

The church was packed to the doors for the crowning. Merlin was there: Arthur had tried hard to seek him out, but he had deliberately avoided the boy and slipped unseen into his place. Arthur must come alone to his crowning; he must step up alone into the King's Seat.

He saw Arthur kneel at the altar. The woollen cloak in which Uther had wrapped him long ago was clasped at his shoulder. The Bishop had set the crown on his head, he had blessed the sword that hung at his side.

Now Arthur rose and stood there, the crowned King. Taking to witness God Himself, the host of heaven, and the company of lords assembled before him, he made his promise of kingship.

"I swear to the people entrusted to my care that they shall have justice. I swear that I will oppose force, tyranny and oppression. I swear that I will work for the well-being of every man, woman and child in my kingdom." The words were spoken with great simplicity. "I swear to defend the Faith. I swear to ratify a peace for my people. The rule of wisdom is a finer thing than the rule of force; I will try to rule wisely and without warfare, but nonetheless I swear to defend my kingdom; for freedom is a greater thing than life. I will rule with justice and with mercy, as befits a ruler, and as befits, above all, a knight."

It was the first time the word had been used in such a way. Arthur the King bound himself to serve his people.

Merlin saw that the younger lords were listening intently. They were prepared to ally themselves with Arthur, and to swear faith as his liegemen. But the older and more powerful men had closed their hearts; they were already seeking arguments against their king. To lay the footings of a new world, Arthur must break down the walls of the old. Was he too young?

With the taking of the oath a new sound had rung through the Church. Fires burn fresh and high in the young, Merlin thought; fierce enough and hard enough to drive a man on. The old had banked their fires against the frost of years.

Could Arthur keep his oath? The young king paused. He said:

"So help me God."

It was noon. Arthur sat in the King's Seat. He waited. Who would come to take the oath of allegiance?

Many of the young lords came. Each swore to be his man, to fight for him and serve him bravely. But most of these young men had no spearsmen, no fortresses, no power.

Welwyn, Lot's young son, knelt at the King's knee; he laid his sword at the King's feet.

"My lord King, I will carry this sword in your honour!" he said. His eyes were full of life and assurance.

"My honour is not so certain a thing, Welwyn. Use your sword against ignorance, and in defence of the oppressed."

Lancelot came forward to the King's Chair and bent his knee. "My lord King, I come to the King's Seat to offer to serve you with all my heart."

"I accept your service gladly. May it never harden the heart you offer."

Two brothers came forward, Balin and Balan. As they walked towards him, Arthur smelled the woods.

They halted in front of the King's Seat and briefly bowed their heads. "Sir, we are here," Balin said.

"I thank you both for coming," said Arthur.

In those few words Balin and Balan had pledged their allegiance to the King, and he had accepted it. They were his men.

Kay came, and Hector came with him. Leodogran came. Others came. But few of them had men or lands to back the King's cause.

Baldwin did not come. Nayntres did not come. The hours went by, and many of the most powerful men in the kingdom had not come. They had turned against Arthur the King. His oath threatened them: they were the lords of the land, and the peasants, the serfs, the slaves, existed only to serve them. This crazy young man had promised to work for the well-being of the people. Who would pay the price?—themselves, the lords and chieftains. They had ridden off in a rage, with a single thought in their heads: they meant to dislodge this dangerous young man, with his spend-thrift promises, from the King's Seat.

Ulfius, who had offered himself as counsellor to King Arthur, watched in concern. "My lord King," he whispered in dismay, "Uther had three men for every one in your ranks!"

Arthur nodded briefly. He refused to show anxiety. Merlin had taught him to show the world a confident face.

"It is quality, not quantity that matters!" he said.

He rose to walk to the King's Hall for the crowning feast. As he walked down the passage, a small skinny fellow sprang from a dark corner. Bending his knee, he looked at the King.

"Lord King, take me into your service. Every king has a jester—let me be yours. My name is Guy."

Arthur considered Guy. He was pleased by what he saw. The jester had bright clear eyes, quick with mockery, but a sad and melancholy mouth.

44

"You will need a jester, my lord. The King's Seat is a lonely place."

"Very well. At the moment there are many things I need more than a jester, but I will take you into my service on trial."

For a moment the thin comical face lost its light-hearted mockery. Arthur was suddenly conscious of the jester's warmth and friendship.

"Thank you, my lord King," Guy said. He looked at the King with grave eyes. Then his face changed as swiftly as if he had pulled on a mask. "I'll use my nonsense to amuse you, and give you the benefit of my advice into the bargain."

Arthur walked on down the passage to the King's Hall with a jester, not an army, at his heels.

Heedless of his overlord's opinion of the young King, Cynric called together his men. There were eighteen in all, two to each horse. Some of them carried a lance or an old sword; others were armed with bow and arrows. Rough wooden shields hung from the horses' necks.

Cynric sat upright in the saddle. "To Arthur the King!" he called. He turned to wave farewell to his wife. She smiled through her tears; her husband led his small shabby force proudly forward.

"Dry your tears!" he called. "It's a fine thing to stand at the young King's side. We are riding out to win glory. We will come home in victory!"

A last wave, and he was away through the gateway. He rode out in a worn leather tunic; his head was bare; but he looked as fine and proud as if he were wearing splendid armour.

"Shove up a bit," one of the men muttered to his companion. "This horse's backside is so broad that my legs are sticking straight out."

"He's a high-stepper," another mocked.

"I only want to ease my seat."

Cynric rode on at the head of his threadbare force. It was a long and dangerous journey, his pouch was empty, but the sun was shining and he would pack his pouch brim-full of adventuring before he came riding home.

The horses jogged patiently on, each with two riders on its back.

Arthur the King walked through the camp. The tents were pitched in ragged rows beyond the city walls. The soldiers had spent day after day waiting wearily; they sprawled round their campfires, roasting haunches of meat, stirring broth and telling tall stories.

The King paused, as usual, to speak to the lords and men he met.

"You should not do that," Ulfius had said. "A king should keep his distance."

"As long as the men are willing to fight for me, they have the right to know me!" Arthur had replied. And even Ulfius had come to admit that these walks through the camp were valuable, linking the King and his men as close as hearth-companions; they would fight the more fiercely at his side.

This time the King paused by a small campfire. He had noticed that these men were new to the camp.

"Where are you from?" he asked as he came towards the fire.

"Well may you ask!" answered one, a man called Geawlin, blind in one eye. He had no idea to whom he was speaking. "We've been on the road for twenty days. My backside is like leather."

Arthur smiled. "A long ride."

"As you say, my lord. We are Cynric's men."

Arthur glanced round the group. The men were dressed in little more than rags. A few skin-and-bone horses grazed in the background. A weathered tent had been pitched a little further on under a tree; it had no banners, no fringing. A soldier was sitting there.

"Is that Cynric?"

"Aye, it is, my lord. We've come bringing nothing but our pride, begging and hunting for food as we went along.

When all else failed, we poached some rabbits or stole a pig—but we had to come!"

The King looked at the small group of men. He was

deeply moved. These men had ridden for twenty days to rally at his standard. Could one find a greater proof of loyalty? What had driven them to set out on this journey?

"My lord, do you know the King?" asked a cripple.

"Yes, I know the King," said Arthur.

"Is it true what they say about him?"

"That depends on what they are saying."

"They say that he is young, but wiser than any other man. They say that he walks through the camp and talks to the common people. They say that his sword is invincible. They say—they say a new time is coming. Is it true, my lord, that the young king defeated Pellinore himself in single combat—and that Pellinore then knelt at his knee to become his man? Is it true that the sword Excalibur was given to him by Merlin, the holy man?"

"You ask a great many questions, my friend," said Arthur the King. "I have met the King. I know him well enough to be certain that he will be glad of your coming!"

"Better tell Cynric that," Geawlin said. "When he saw the camp his courage failed him. We have no fine armour, my lord. We don't even have a standard. People pointed us out, grinned, asked us if we were wayfarers who'd missed our road—"

Arthur raised his hand to check him. "The King rates courage far above fine armour. He does not prize clothes, equipment or gear, he only cares for courage, strength and loyalty."

"Then the King is a wise man."

Cynric had risen and come over to them. "What are you looking for?" he asked curiously.

"I bring you a message from Arthur the King," Arthur said with a smile. "He asks that you and your men attend him this evening to make your duty to him."

"But I . . . We have come a long road. Our clothes are in rags . . ."

48

"I have already told your men that the King pays little heed to outward appearances. Come as you are!"

The King's Hall was crowded; one by one the lords were called forward for a few brief moments of private talk with the King. He questioned them about their equipment and about the strength of their forces; he listened to their complaints and grievances. Some were magnificently dressed, rose-scarlet cloaks flaring over bright mail; others were in plain warrior gear. The Hall was lit by a blaze of pine torches. Servants were carrying round great pitchers of beer.

As the great doors swung open, the King looked up. Everyone turned to watch.

A young man came in. His tunic was torn, his leather shoes covered in dust.

Behind him came eighteen men, dressed in rags. One of them was lame, but he carried his axe none the less. Another had lost an eye; the right-hand side of his face was puckered by a scar.

They stopped just inside the doors, glancing round uneasily.

"Come closer," called the King. The Hall fell quiet, though here and there men made mocking comments—"Who are those scarecrows?"

"Come closer!" Did the King too want to amuse himself?

"Go on, the King is calling you."

Slowly, uncertainly, the tattered group moved forward.

"By my one eye . . . it's that lad!" whispered Geawlin.

"You are welcome to the King's Hall, Cynric," said Arthur the King.

There was no mockery in his voice. Many of the lords exchanged glances. This scarecrow band . . . and yet the King greeted them so courteously. Perhaps the joke was still to come?

The King had risen. He paused, considering, weighing his words; then he spoke directly to Cynric, but also beyond him, to every man in his Hall.

"You have ridden a twenty-day road to come here, undergoing great hardships to reach this Hall. You have gone against your overlord. For my sake you have left hearth and home. Neither knowing me, nor in any hope of gain, you have come this long road to show that you are the King's true men. You have staked this on my cause, Cynric; I rate that stake very high. Any man who mocks you because your equipment is simple and workaday belittles my Hall and my honour. The army marches in the morning. You and your men will ride in Pellinore's squadron. I appoint you to my bodyguard. I thank you for coming."

"My lord King—" Cynric bent his knee and his men knelt behind him. The cripple stumbled; a companion prodded him and he righted himself hastily.

"My lord King, whatever we have is yours."

A murmur rose in the great Hall. Who was this Cynric? Why had he been so greatly honoured?

Guy, the little court jester, had been watching breathlessly. He sprang forward to mock himself.

"King Arthur," he cried. "I too want to show myself a hero. Cynric has travelled for—what? twenty days? *I* have travelled all my life to reach you—and I have suffered cuffs and kicks. Let me too join your body-guard!"

A roar of laughter rang through the hall. Everybody was watching skinny little Guy. Arthur laughed too. He was grateful to his jester for having made light of his own speech to Cynric. High words, but necessary ones—

"Are you truly a hero, Guy?"

"Certainly I am a hero, my lord King—but perhaps not in the attack. I shall have to be a hero who doesn't go storming walls."

"I need the kind of men who will help me to *build*

a kingdom," Arthur said, "not merely to storm the enemy's strongholds." He signed to his servants and once more the beer went round.

Merlin sat writing. He described the crowning and the fierce struggle which was to follow:

The force which King Arthur had assembled was not a strong one. The enemy had far more men than he. But his was a close-knit army, an army which was aware of the greatness of its young king, and which had gained some insight into the ideals for which he fought.

6

The King Goes to War

King Arthur's army was ready to march. The Bishop
and the priests walked through the ranks to bless the
kneeling men.

The King was watching from the top of a hill. He
saw the Lord of Wadesham, kneel for blessing—but on
Wadesham's breast was a bear's claw, an amulet which
he believed would make him invincible in battle and
defend him against the powers of darkness. Wadesham
treated his servants without humanity and punished
them cruelly for any fault; yet he was the King's true
man and would fight bravely in the King's cause.

There knelt Brian, who had told the King his services
must be paid for with a grant of land. "I cannot bargain
with the kingdom's peace," Arthur had said; furious,
Brian had exclaimed that he would not serve for charity's
sake. But he had stayed none the less, hoping to take
rebel prisoners whose kin would ransom them at great
price.

There knelt Welwyn. His head was stuffed with
dreams. He was a flourisher, jaunty as a cock;
but he would keep his word. He was the King's
true man.

Kay knelt there, Pellinore, Balin and Balan whose
lack of grace and eloquence was more than outweighed
by their stubborn courage.

There knelt Abbot Theodorus, in hauberk and helmet.
A man could not be true warrior and true priest;

time and again Theodorus had drawn his sword and ridden out to enrich his abbey.

Lancelot knelt also. Arthur hoped that the coming battle would not destroy his humanity.

The trumpets rang out in the signal for departure. Arthur the King rode up to the Bishop to take his leave.

"My lord King," said the priest, sounding troubled, "I pray God you will not under-rate the enemy's strength."

"I ride out in the full assurance of victory."

"Go then, my lord King, and may your faith keep you!"

The army waited for a sign. After a dragging march which had lasted week after week, they were at last face to face with the enemy, whose army was drawn up on a hill opposite. The king saw their mail flash in the sun.

Pellinore rode up, to halt in front of the King. "We are ready!"

The King nodded. His host stood ready for battle. He saw Cynric in his new armour: the young soldier shifted in his saddle, called something to his men, settled his helmet more firmly on his head. Welwyn sat proudly erect, his face alive with eagerness; Lancelot was fingering the strap of his shield.

Arthur glanced from one to the other. A young spearman's lips moved nervously; an experienced soldier grinned and, raising his battle-axe, called something to his neighbour.

The army was ready, only waiting for a sign. Arthur had spoken in plain terms of why they must make war. His men would stand firm. Even the least-brave would be swept along, shivering and afraid, by the courage of their companions, until they too forgot themselves in the struggle for life or death.

The Lord of Wadesham tightened his reins. He would ride out, to live or die, in the hope of spoil.

Arthur gripped the hilt of his sword Excalibur. For a

moment he thought of Merlin. Was this sword truly invincible? The enemy's army was far greater than his own—Then he drew the bright sword and raised it high above his head.

"Forward—for King Arthur, for Britain!" Pellinore cried in a great voice.

"Forward, for King Arthur and for Britain!"

The shout rang round the valley. The army began to advance. Arthur the King rode forward at the head of the closed ranks, into his first battle and into the terrors of the battlefield.

"Forward, for King Arthur and for Britain!"

The battle-cry still rang out across the field, although bitter fighting had gone on for hours.

The men struggled on: slashing and thrusting: their courage as bright and steadfast as ever. Clouds of dust hung over the field. The clash of swords and the screaming of horses mingled with the cries of the wounded and the dying. Fallen shields and splintered lances lay tumbled everywhere. The earth was drenched with blood. Wounded men cried out for mercy, but the horsemen charged forward across the bodies of the fallen, living and dead alike, to clash again with the enemy. Welwyn had hacked his way deep into the enemy ranks and survived only because Balin and Balan spurred their horses on in his wake, and saved his reckless life.

Cynric held his place at the King's side. Other men might thrust forward to break the enemy ranks and win the honours of war; but he was the King's bodyguard, his duty was to ride at the King's thigh.

The arrows came hissing like rain to pierce the soldiers' mail-shirts. Lances bit through leather and flesh. Axe and sword crashed down on skull and fist.

It was a fierce and bloody fight. The two hosts struggled together, blindly ramming forward with lance and axe and sword to avenge their fallen companions.

Sweat streamed from the soldiers and horses, mingling with the blood and the dust.

Arthur glimpsed Baldwin of Brittany through the clash and surge of the battle. He rode straight for him, Cynric driving forward at his side.

The two men struck mightily at one another. Under the pounding blows Baldwin's shield shattered; his sword snapped off short in his hand. He tried to wheel his horse round, but Cynric had cut off his retreat. He shouted angrily to his men for help, but the cry was drowned in the roar of battle. Cynric caught his horse's rein, and the King swung up Excalibur to strike. And Baldwin, surrendering, allowed himself to be led away.

Lancelot fought bravely and resolutely, but again and again some small, precise glimpse sprang out from the terrible confusion of the battle and made him shiver: a cripple leaping awkwardly forward to cover a friend who had been blinded in one eye; a spearman with an arrow stuck deep in his shoulder, still defending a dying companion; a riderless horse, standing, quiet and still, beside a fallen warrior. Each roused a spring of tears in him. He wept for the small brave sacrifices of the world.

"Forward—for King Arthur and for Britain!"

For hours the rebels held firm. They had been promised great rewards—and the spoils of victory would be greater still. But at last, when Baldwin had been led away, when the sun was low, their resistance broke.

The battlefield echoed with cheers: the enemy was giving ground.

Trumpets shrilled across the field. Nayntres the King fell back with his horsemen; Cambenic and his men followed, a number of loyal soldiers struggling to cover their withdrawl. Broken, disordered, the enemy retreated.

Pellinore roared out across the field. He had removed his dented helmet and battered it into shape again; now, clapping it on, he called on his troops to harry the retreat.

But the foot-soldiers were drawn with fatigue; they propped themselves up with shield and sword. Some men just stood there, sweating, fighting for breath; others sank to the ground. Silent, shuddering and exhausted, the King's men tried to pull themselves together. They had been outnumbered by almost three to one, but victory was theirs.

Arthur had taken off his helmet. He rode slowly across the field of battle. He had sent Pellinore, Cynric and the others back to camp; he wanted to be alone as he rode out across the terrible field.

He reined in his horse. There lay John, Lord of Wadesham, his helmet shattered. His eyes, still open, stared up coldly; the eyes of a man who looked on a strange country. The King dismounted and knelt beside him. Gently he removed the shattered helmet. He gazed down at the bear's claw that lay on the dead man's breast. Lord John's conduct had befitted a man who wore such a badge; he had been as strong and savage as the creature whose claw he treasured. But he had not known the ways of the heart. He had died in ignorance.

King Arthur drew the lids down over the staring eyes. He rode on. A dying man called out to him, and again he dismounted. "My lord, the devils are coming for me!" The young man's face was haggard with fear. He was seeing the images of Hell.

"They will not come, my friend," Arthur said. "God is a God of love."

"If God were love—"

The boy's gaze seemed to clear. Arthur raised him against his knee and held him as he died.

King Arthur rode on across the battlefield, looking down at the dead and the dying. Wounded horses were being slaughtered for meat. The dead lay heaped together. Seeing them, the King longed to ride on and leave the world behind him. Merlin had done so—But instead he turned his horse and rode back to the camp.

He must take his place in the King's Seat. The people were in his charge and he must care for them.

For weeks, for months, the army was kept on the march, although the King set his face against unnecessary killing, preferring to win by patient tactful argument. If all such efforts failed, his men would storm the rebel stronghold or fight the rebel force in the open field, the young King riding at the head of his troops, sword in hand. Word of Excalibur had already spread: men fell back in fear at the first blows from the sword.

Day followed day as they marched on, passing Roman villas long-deserted, burnt-out farm steadings, the scorched and trampled fields of the peasants. The people slipped away to hide in ditches and copses until the army had passed. They had hidden their cows, horses and sheep in the woods, for soldiers were always hungry and would seize whatever came to hand. But one morning the King's men found a man, standing dazed before the ruins of his burnt-out steading, with a tired wife and

some ragged children hiding behind him. Cambenic's
men had been at work here. The man had fallen on his
knees before the King. Not knowing to whom he spoke,
he had begged for mercy and pity.

"My lord, we are men like yourself . . . we are capable
of suffering like you!" Tears had been pouring down his
face.

Arthur instructed Cynric and his men to rebuild the
steading. He stocked the place with cows and sheep from
the army train. As he rode on, the man ran beside his
horse, praying for God's blessing on the King and
shouting praises until Arthur, sickened by the words,
ordered him home.

The King's army and Cambenic's clashed at last, and
in the fighting Cambenic was killed. His son came to
surrender his sword. He came in the full expectation that
he would be made to pay for his father's actions. But,
instead, the King made him his man.

"Your people are exhausted," said the King. "They
worked hard to make a living, but your father took all
they had. You are exploiting your people, who carry
your burdens. The world regards them as creatures of
small account, but you—you should respect them."

The boy flushed as he listened.

"Your land lies within my kingdom. Rule it justly and
in peace. I will show you no mercy if you break your
word."

Arthur the King made young Cambenic swear an
oath in the presence of his men.

"I will not plunder the house of God. I will not strike
His priests. I will not steal my neighbour's ox, nor his
cow, nor his sheep, nor any of his beasts. I will not rob,
nor help to rob, any man. I will rule justly. I will temper
justice with mercy."

When Cambenic had taken the oath, the King laid
his father's sword across his wrists.

"I will serve you faithfully, my lord King," the young man said.

The army marched on into the north. They defeated the Pictish tribes and drove back the Scots beyond the Eagles' Wall.

Nayntres, King of Garloth, knew that Arthur was a man of peace. He came to meet him with a small group of followers and tried to flatter the young king, whom once he had called a cox-comb; he offered himself as the King's servant. But Arthur knew there was no faith in Nayntres, and dismissing him, he set Cynric in his Seat as Lord of Garloth.

It was a warm and quiet night. The King sat in his tent, listening to the sounds of the camp borne on the wind: horses stamping in the picket lines, men singing as they sat round a campfire and threw the dice:

"My sweetheart's mouth is warm and soft,
Her breath is heaven's breath;
But I stood on the battlefield
And saw the scythman Death.
My sweetheart's mouth is Paradise
There journey's end should be;
No girl ever lay in Death's bone-arms—
He swung his scythe at me—"

"Stop that noise there," shouted Pellinore, who could not get to sleep. King Arthur smiled unwillingly. He felt depressed and tired. It had taken two years of fierce fighting, but at last his kingdom lay in peace. The rebels had come to kneel at his knee. He must parry the Saxon raids, but once that was done he could begin to rebuild his kingdom. He was the High King now, and the thought weighed heavy on him.

A slight rustle made him look up. Mouse-quiet, Guy had appeared in the opening of the tent.

"Why don't you sleep, my lord High King?"

"What about you, Guy? You are not sleeping either."

"My conscience will not let me sleep. How can I sleep when my conscience is awake?" Guy said at once. "But like everybody else I must make the best of it."

King Arthur sighed. "I am tired of rowing against the current, Guy."

"That's what Noah said after he'd been bobbing up and down in his ark for days!"

Guy hesitated. Dared he speak his mind?

"But Noah's situation was different from yours, my lord King."

"How so, Guy?"

"They entered the ark two by two: the birds, the deer, the snakes, the pigs, the mammoths. And—the people, too." Guy took a deep breath. "You are alone, my lord King."

"I should dearly like to marry, Guy. But I must devote myself to my kingdom. How could I . . ." The King gazed out into the night. It was true: he longed for a wife. For two long years he had lived on the march. The days had been filled with councils of war, with administering justice, with guiding his lords. But sometimes, as now, in the quiet evenings, a longing for a wife, for love, filled him.

Could he consider marrying? As he marched through the country with his army, he had realized time and again the terrible conditions under which men still lived in the far, wild corners of his kingdom. Settlements made war on one another; women were carried off or won on the throw of the dice; children were sold; a trivial argument over hunting- or fishing-rights was settled, only too often, by bloody fighting. The people lived in caves and lean-to shelters, terrified and superstitious. What else could one expect: their cattle were stolen, their strips of ground trampled by hunting parties, their huts burnt down. Many of them had spent their whole lives working without pause. No one cared for them or defended them. They could only endure.

The task of bringing the people a better and gentler life was immense. Could he think of marriage before he had fulfilled even this one part of his calling?

"My lord King, an armed man, a swordsman, can never cut his way to happiness. But a lover may win in peace the country of the heart."

Guy slipped away. Left alone, the King rose and went outside. To the left of his tent some guards were sitting by a smouldering fire. One of them again began to sing:

"My sweetheart's mouth is Paradise,
There journey's end should be—"

The stars were bright in a clear sky. It promised to be a warm day tomorrow.

7

Guinevere

Merlin was writing at the table-board.

"Arthur had made war and won peace for his kingdom. He had now to consolidate that peace. It was a task full of disappointments and set-backs. It could only be carried through by a man who had a loving woman at his side. I looked all over Britain for such a woman. At last I found her in the stronghold of Leodogran the King."

Through the small window Merlin stared out at the dark night. He saw again Guinevere, Leodogran's daughter. Her eyes were as tranquil as still water. Her mouth was tender, mobile and sensitive. Her skin was clear. She was a woman of great beauty, a woman to love; but more than this, thought Merlin, she had a strength to shape and make a man.

Merlin had sought her and found her. The rest was simple. He sent word to the Saxon chief, Ceowulf, that great treasure lay stored in Leodogran's stronghold. He sent word to Leodogran, warning him of the coming Saxon attack. He knew that Leodogran would call upon King Arthur for help. And Arthur would come.

Would his heart quicken when he saw Guinevere in her beauty? Merlin was sure that it would do so.

The Saxon chief Ceowulf besieged Leodogran's stronghold. The king refused to surrender. No offer of ransom was made, and Ceowulf accordingly ordered his men to attack. Under cover of immense shields, the Saxons brought up their ladders. At that moment one of the look-outs came running up, out of breath.

"Ceowulf, lord, see, over there—"

He pointed to the hills. A great cloud of dust was rising on the wind. With an experienced eye Ceowulf calculated that over a hundred riders were coming at full gallop. He could not withstand such an attack. He ordered his men to break ranks, make for cover, and try to reach the warships that lay off-shore.

Ceowulf sprang to the stirrup. His men ran for their lives, hoping to escape by plunging into the dark wood near the stronghold. Few of them reached it. There came the first riders, led by King Arthur, with Lancelot and Welwyn by his side. His orders rang out crisp and clear above the thudding of the horses' hooves. In an instant his force had split to hunt down the Saxons, cutting across their lines of flight. Excalibur flashed in the sun.

Leodogran's young daughter was watching from the walls. She saw the King with the bright sword in his hand, and her heart quickened.

Within a few hours the battle was over. Only a handful of the Saxons stood to fight. Ceowulf had ridden straight at King Arthur with the courage of despair, but the King's first blow struck the sword from his hand. The Saxon was taken prisoner.

Leodogran greeted King Arthur in the courtyard of his stronghold. "High King, I am your servant."

"We have a long ride behind us," said King Arthur. "My men and I would be glad to rest here." He made to follow Leodogran into the Great Hall. But suddenly he paused. He looked into a girl's great eyes. He noticed the white throat, the silver band in the thick dark golden hair. He saw her smile. She had a generous, tender mouth. Was this where paradise lay, as the soldier had sung?

"These are my daughters, my lord the High King."

Arthur greeted all four, but it was the hand of the youngest girl that he held the longest.

"My daughter Guinevere."

It was a singing name. The sunlight blazed about her. Something Merlin had said long ago came back to him and he saw that it was true: lovers were given a different world, a shining place to walk in.

His sadness seemed to have lifted abruptly. With a light and singing heart he sat at the King's Board in the Great Hall. Leodogran spread a feast for his rescuers. Fires blazed under ovens and spits in the kitchen. Dish after dish was carried into the Hall: highly seasoned mutton, roast sucking pig, crisp pasties.

It was a long time since Lancelot, Welwyn and the others had seen the King so exuberant.

King Arthur questioned his host cautiously about his plans for his daughters.

"My three elder daughters have been promised in marriage," said Leodogran, "but I want to keep my youngest, Guinevere, under my own roof-tree a little longer."

Arthur's heart sang with the name. He stayed on in the stronghold for some days, and time and again sought a chance to be alone with her.

The night before his departure, he slept badly, dreaming of his kingdom. He was riding slowly through a desolate country: through dark woods, past barren rocks where the wind came keening off the sea. The past was all about him; godless, inhuman, shifting so that he talked with rebel chieftains, fought against invaders, judged disputes, founded churches and monasteries. Even in his dreams he was conscious of his longing to teach his lords the ways of knighthood and gather the great men of the kingdom under his roof-tree. But now, among these familiar images, Guinevere came walking into his dream.

Guinevere. Dreaming still, Arthur fought grimly on through rank after rank of Saxons, Picts, Scots; he beat off wolves; he put down the rebel lords. Exhausted, he came at last to an inland water, still among ferns. He stripped off his armour and walked to the water-side. Guinevere stood there, lovely among the green. He took his sweetheart in his arms. This was his journey's end.

Early in the morning he was wakened by a servant. A messenger had come from Pellinore, asking the King to return to the camp at once, as quickly as horse would bear him. Two of the lords had quarrelled; such a dispute could split the army.

That morning King Arthur galloped back to the camp. The world was singing round him. For before he left he had declared his love for Guinevere, and King Leodogran had given him his daughter's hand.

Merlin stood in front of his hut in the woods. He heard the thud of a horse's hooves and he knew who was coming.

Arthur had ridden out from the King's House to bring news of his coming marriage.

The King rode at a walking pace, looking around him at the familiar woods. This was the country of his childhood, full of memories.

Some weeks ago he had set up his household in a great stronghold called Camelot. The war was over. The lords had ridden home to their own lands, taking their men with them. Only a few had stayed in the King's House, to help Arthur rebuild his kingdom.

Merlin knew that it was easier to make war than to consolidate peace. Was the king perhaps coming also to ask for advice?

66

"Welcome, my lord King!"

They sat down on the seat in front of the hut. They spoke of secret matters. King Arthur told his old tutor about the campaign which had just ended, about the setting up of his household, and, last, about his love for Guinevere.

"Next week I shall send Lancelot to fetch her. And that is the beginning of a new life. Such great happiness will lighten the cares of government."

Merlin shook his head. "Perfect happiness is a brittle thing, my lord King—too brittle to pursue. For every hour of high happiness a lover spends an hour of darkness and depression."

Arthur laughed. "My happiness runs high as a river in flood."

Merlin did not reply at once. He stared into the wood. "Sometimes rivers run dry, my lord King. Sometimes they burst their banks. Sometimes they silt up, sometimes they are strong enough and swift enough to wear away the hardest rocks. Your happiness runs high now—but it cannot do so for ever."

The old man leant back against the wall of his hut, paused, and then said, "But every river at last makes its way to the open sea. Journey's end."

King Arthur gave his old tutor a penetrating look. Surely every living man sought for happiness?

Merlin smiled. He was himself again.

"If you can find a single man in all your kingdom, Arthur, who has found true and lasting happiness, I will become your jester!" He had dropped the royal title now, and his voice sounded as it used to do. The conversation took a different turn. King Arthur began to talk about the lords: they still could not understand what he strove for, and he admitted that sometimes he despaired.

It was late in the afternoon when at last he turned to go.

"The river runs at floodtide, Merlin," he called when

he took his leave. His voice rang out through the wood, exuberant and light-hearted.

"Don't run so high that the banks burst, my lord King," Merlin called after him.

He did not move until the young King had disappeared from sight; then he went into his hut, set the parchments on the table, and began to write:

Young Lancelot was among the bravest and finest of the men in the King's Household, and Arthur the King loved him above all others. He gave Lancelot the honour of journeying in the King's name to bring back his bride from her father's Hall.

Lancelot was the King's true man. But neither the King nor Lancelot himself could foresee the consequences of this task. I saw what was to come, but nevertheless had to play my appointed part—

"Have you ever been in love, Guy?" Arthur looked at his jester. The question was lightly asked but must be answered. For a moment Guy let drop his mask and his eyes lost their habitual mockery. Briefly he saw his young wife; lived again their first meeting in the market place: a girl as fresh as the apples she was selling, with a colour in her face as warm as theirs. But leprosy had dulled her freshness. It had fed on her as a worm feeds on an apple, slowly eating away all that Guy had held dearest in life.

Had he ever been in love! A jester was a man too, wasn't he?

They had gone out from the city together, leaving its crowded world behind them. He had earned a living by showing his tricks with a dancing bear, and by selling jokes. But little by little the disease ate through her. By the end her face was the face of a different woman. The sight of it had sickened him.

"We have met, love and I," he said now. His voice was flippant and gay.

"Only a few more days and she will be here, Guy. The waiting time hangs heavy. I find myself counting the hours."

"A man's heart is impatient. It runs ahead of time," said Guy. It was his duty to keep the king amused, but his wife's image stayed with him still.

"Was your girl beautiful, Guy?"

But Guy could never tell the King the truth. If he told the king of his love, and of what had happened to her, Arthur would never feel free to laugh at his jokes again.

Had she been beautiful? Yes, she had been beautiful for a short space; Guy could not talk of it.

But the King was impatient for his bride's coming: it was his jester's duty to make the waiting time seem shorter.

"They say that all cats are grey at night, my lord King!" Guy said, bent on talking nonsense.

"And did you catch your cat in the dark?" King Arthur laughed. Guy felt the life-blood draining from his heart. He heard the warning clatter of the leper's rattle his young wife had had to carry.

"Love turned me into a cat too," he said, "a prowling tom stalking the roof-tree."

He made a grimace, and the King smiled. The jester was tossing out nonsense to shorten the waiting time for his master.

On his coming to Leodogran's Hall, Lancelot gave Guinevere the King's messages, and with proper courteous words put into her hands the gifts the King had sent her. He spoke with Leodogran too, and presented to him the gifts the King had sent as tokens of friendship.

Now everything was ready for the journeying. At the head of a crowd of attendants, Lancelot and Guinevere rode out through the great gateway. It was May, and spring sunlight lay across the hills. Guinevere was light-hearted and gay. The King's people treated her with infinite respect and honour, and this delighted her. She had grown up, year after year, in the strict seclusion of her father's Hall; now she saw a new world opening out, attendant on her pleasure.

The journey to the King's House was a long one, but for Guinevere the days were flying. Lancelot served her with the greatest courtesy, attentive to her smallest wish. He was the first man with whom she had been in company for any length of time. Talking and laughing, they rode together day after day. Sometimes they rode ahead, leaving their retinue far behind them. Sometimes they let their horses drop to a walk and lagged behind, meaning no harm. Sometimes he gathered flowers for her—"from my lord the High King".

One bright morning Guinevere impulsively swung aside from the path they were following and galloped forward through the silent wood. When she reached a clear stream, she dismounted to drink. Courteous as ever, Lancelot knelt to cup his hands and offer her the water.

They laughed when they saw their reflections in the water; two heads bending close together. Guinevere bent further forward, and for an instant lost her balance, and Lancelot caught her back. Briefly she lay in his arms. She was no longer laughing: the light-hearted words, the casual gaiety had gone. His mouth was on hers. He knew that he loved her.

They were shaken and appalled. They let go of one another and remounted without a word; and still without a word rode back to their companions.

Did it matter so greatly? It cost Lancelot his peace of mind. He could not break faith with the King; he could not dishonour their friendship. But he could not forget Guinevere's eyes as she looked up into his face.

Guinevere: surely, he thought, once they reached the

court the excitement of a new world would rub out her brief affection for him. The finest man in the kingdom would be hers, and she would surely come to love the King. But he knew that he himself would never be heart-whole again. He must live all his days with a great longing for the woman who was the King's wife.

In a few days the journey would be over. He tried to talk himself into forgetting Guinevere, into putting her out of his mind. But he could not do it; his love was deaf to reasoning. Hers was a singing name, and his head sang with it.

8

The Knights of the Round Table

The greatest in the kingdom came to attend the marriage of Arthur and Guinevere.

Lancelot was standing close by the altar. He looked around the crowded church. Old Ulfius was clearly moved. Iloide, who had been given a place of honour, had caught Hector's hand. She gazed silently and wonderingly at the young couple. Cynric sat behind her, and Welwyn was there too, carefree and light-hearted.

The Bishop was praying aloud. His voice was grave as he asked God to bless the marriage. Lancelot looked at the King, kneeling beside Guinevere at the altar, and a strange emotion caught at his heart. He looked on a man who was his lord, his king, his friend, his hearth-companion, and, more than this, a pattern by which he must make his own life.

The Bishop had finished speaking. The King raised his head.

"I do. So help me God." The King had given his word.

Lancelot looked at Guinevere. Ever since their coming to Camelot he had avoided her. Had she, in the excitement of life in the King's House, forgotten the moment by the water-side? He hoped so with all his heart.

"I do. So help me God." She too had given her word.

The King gave Guinevere his arm and led her slowly through the church. The crowd was shouting and cheering outside. Their eyes were full of hope as they watched the young couple.

72

Merlin pulled the hood of a homespun pilgrim's cloak deep over his eyes. Being tall, he could see easily over the heads of the crowd. Arthur and Guinevere stood there, each meaning to love and cherish the other, to comfort and care for the people, to keep the kingdom safe and secure. He longed to spare them all sorrow and disappointment. For a moment he was tempted to call out to them, to tell them to close their eyes to all difficulties. But he was silent. Like Lancelot, like Welwyn, Arthur and Guinevere must walk out into the dark.

Merlin knew, in general terms, what was to come. He knew that Arthur the King was soon to found a new order of knighthood. The men of that order would be true knights, made after the pattern he had drawn for Arthur: men who would be brave and honest, true and merciful.

He glanced round. The people were cheering wildly. For a moment all the world seemed in tune: Arthur was young, strong, blazing with happiness; Guinevere was beautiful, and fresh, enchanted by her new life.

But there was Lancelot. His heart would over-master him. There was Welwyn: his head was stuffed with dreams. There, in their gay cloaks, stood the men who were to be the King's knights; and Merlin knew what would happen to each and every one. And yet the King's order of knighthood would make the world a finer place. It would widen men's apprehension of God. It would give their lives a new brightness. And there stood the King. Whatever happened, he would endure; Merlin himself had taught him endurance.

The marriage feast was in full swing. The lords and their wives were seated at the great round table. Servants hurried to and fro, bringing dish after dish. Singers and tumblers were performing to please the guests.

Halfway through the feast the King rose. Ulfius shouted for silence, and the noise was hushed. Startled, the lords listened as the King spoke about his kingdom and the course of his reign. He announced that he meant to found a new Order.

"I am creating the Order of the Round Table. I do so for the sake of peace, for the well-being of the people, for the establishment of the rule of law. Each knight may win his own seat at this table by helping those who are oppressed, by fighting for those who are helpless, by being merciful to the weak."

Welwyn sprang up. "Yes, yes, I swear I shall do so!" he exclaimed recklessly. His eyes were blazing with self-confidence.

"Yes, we swear it!" the other lords echoed, anxious not to lag behind.

Guy was looking at the King, at the lords and their wives, at all the servants who had lined up along the walls. He noticed that Guinevere secretly held out her hand under the table-board. The King felt her touch and closed his hand over hers.

There was complete silence in the Great Hall of Camelot as King Arthur announced his aims for the new Order. He spoke of his knights as servants. He spoke of striving for peace. He spoke of courage and wisdom, strength and justice.

"Any man who is willing to devote himself in this way to the remaking of this kingdom will be confirmed as a knight of the Round Table, and will have the right to use the title 'Sir' before his name."

A murmur arose. Guy saw that Welwyn was about to jump up again, but Balan, who was sitting next to him, pulled him back. "Think before you speak," Balan murmured; and Welwyn kept his seat.

Lancelot stared down at the King's Board. He was perhaps the only one to understand the full meaning of the words.

Guy turned then to look at Modred, who was now the King's brother-in-law. Modred was a hard man, ambitious, and sharper-witted than any other. He cared nothing for other men's feelings. Was it possible for such a man to be the King's true servant?

"Let the wine go round once more!" called King Arthur. He nodded to Guy who sprang forward to mock the company. The solemn mood had been broken. The singing rang out again. Laughter echoed round the Hall. Nobody noticed that Modred sat watching the King with deep and bitter envy.

The lords and the servants had withdrawn. The marriage feast was over. Arthur lay in the King's great bed and took his young queen in his arms. He murmured her name. Her mouth was soft on his. The soldier's song sang in his head.

9

Ready at the Stirrup

With his lords around him, Arthur sat in the King's Chair. As usual, a stream of people had been called before him: peasants with grievances, a woman accused of witchcraft, a man who had stolen some sheep.

Sometimes bored, sometimes amused or intrigued, the King's household listened to his decisions.

A tenant farmer, his hair dishevelled, his face unwashed, fell to his knees before the King's Seat. He fidgeted with his cap and hardly dared to look up. But then, abruptly, he plucked up courage. His voice shook as he made his plea.

"My lord King Arthur, you must help me! I cut the hay and took it to my master. I harvested the corn for the Convent. On Palm Sunday I paid the sheep-tax, and on St. Denis's Day I delivered ten pigs to the Lord of Brodeshead. I have faithfully brought in the timber and paid my dues. I have paid the Lord of Brodeshead for the use of the mill and have given my eldest daughter into service in his Hall. And now, my lord King, the harvest has failed, but none the less I am threatened with further levies which I cannot pay. Everything I once owned has been taken from me and—"

"That is enough!"

Startled by the King's voice, the farmer fell silent. He looked helplessly round him.

King Arthur glanced at the men of his household, the

Knights of the Round Table. Sir Modred, his brother-in-law, took a step forward.

"Allow me to investigate this matter for you, my lord King."

Arthur looked at his wife's brother. Modred had a sharp brain, but he lacked grace. And yet he had shown himself a champion of the oppressed, and time and time again he had ridden out to see that the tenants and peasants had justice.

"Ride to Brodeshead, Sir Modred, and look into this matter. Tell the lord of Brodeshead he must live within the law. And tell him too that this is the last warning I will give him."

Sir Modred bowed. As the King's wife's brother and as a Knight of the Round Table, he had become a powerful man. But this did not satisfy him. In greatest secrecy, he had laid plans with a number of discontented lords. He would ride out as the King's envoy but he would take the opportunity of enmeshing Brodeshead in his plot. Brodeshead was not a powerful man, but every ally counted. That was what Modred needed: allies, more and more of them, until he was strong enough to strike. Now, with a low bow, he turned to leave the Hall.

Guinevere watched him go. As always when Arthur held court, the place was thronged. Men and women crowded together in their bright garments, with here and there the contrast of a holy man's sombre grey habit. Modred was thrusting his way through with difficulty. How different he was from most of the other knights. How different, in particular, from Lancelot, about whom she now sat thinking. Ever since that bright May morning by the water-side he had avoided her. He had asked Arthur for one mission after another. His name was famous far and wide: Sir Lancelot, the first among the Knights of the Round Table, the King's friend, the King's confidant. But his heart had not changed: he was still the same man, seeing all things in plain simple terms, gentle of temper, and loyal.

She turned to look at King Arthur, her husband. The people admired him, the Knights of the Round Table were devoted to him, his enemies feared him. But Guinevere knew, better than anyone else, that King Arthur had been trapped by his own ideals: his lords confused strength with courage, flattery with friendship. They thought it a fine thing to pick a fight in the name of honour. Again and again she had argued that this was wrong; and her arguments had not helped to make their marriage easy.

One after another the petitioners came to kneel in front of the King's Seat. They came from far and wide to ask Arthur for justice, for help, for support. Again and again, Arthur had to bite back his disappointment as he saw how men throughout the kingdom paid no heed to his laws. Each day there was new word of plundering, rebellion, disloyalty, treason.

Sir Lancelot reined in his horse. On the muddy path in front of him stood two children, dirty and almost naked. They were holding out their hands to beg for alms.

Lancelot had been sent on the King's affairs and was now on his way to the King's House to report. But he had time in hand. He stopped, smiling down at the children.

"Why are you asking for alms?"

"My mother says that every little helps, my lord," said the boy. He came boldly up to the horse, his sister following with some hesitation.

"Are you strong, my lord?" the boy asked. "Have you ever won a fight—a really difficult fight?"

"Yes, I have won sometimes!" said Lancelot and again he smiled at the two. He was always touched by children's innocence. He looked from the boy to the girl.

"I want to be a lady when I grow up," said the girl. Her fair hair hung, dirty and tangled, around her face. "I want to have a blue dress and—"

"Don't be silly," said her brother.

"And what?" asked Lancelot.

"Then I shall ask Sir Lancelot to be my knight!" Her voice was determined and her dark eyes were serious.

"Don't be silly," the boy said again and he pushed his sister aside. Then he looked up.

"Do you know Sir Lancelot, my lord? Have you ever seen him? Is it true that he has never been defeated? What does he look like?"

Lancelot looked down at the two children. They stood

there by his horse, filthy dirty, yet touching and innocent.

"He looks exactly as I do," he said with a smile. "He wears a hauberk and a helmet like mine, and he carries a lance and a shield like mine. Sometimes he rides out on the King's affairs. Sometimes he has to fight men who have failed in their duty. And sometimes, very occasionally—"

The boy looked at him, wide-eyed. "Well, sometimes what?" he asked impatiently.

"Sometimes he reins in his horse and talks to children who are begging for alms."

"Does he give them anything?"

Sir Lancelot nodded. "Yes, he always gives them something." He took out a small gold coin. Then, seeing that the boy was beginning to understand, he said quickly: "Here you are. Here is something to remember Sir Lancelot by—" On the word he set spurs to his horse.

"My lord, my lord—!" The boy's excited voice followed him. "Are you—?"

"I am indeed!" called Lancelot and he rode on, lighter at heart than he had felt before.

At full trot he rode past the steading that was held by Hector and Iloide. Suddenly a thought occurred to him, and reining back, he turned his horse towards the skyline woods. He searched until he found the lonely hut among the leaves. He dismounted, but before he could knock the door opened.

"I have returned again, sir. Since first we chanced to meet I have felt driven to visit you from time to time." He entered the hut and sat down on a wooden seat.

"It's the selfsame tale," he said.

The holy man looked at him consideringly. Sir Lancelot met his gaze. "I promised to serve the King, to be his true man. I have eaten his bread, sat at his hearth, slept in his Hall, fought at his side. He is my lord; more, he is my closest friend. I lost my heart to his wife. And so I journey around the kingdom. My fame increases with every day that passes. Men praise my courage at every turn. But I am empty of hope, because of my love for Guinevere."

The words came pouring out. Then he sat listening to the tranquil words of this old holy man who understood him so well. He had met him years before, by accident, and had walked with him to the hut in the woods. He had stared in amazement at the books and manuscripts shelved around the walls. This strange old man seemed to know everything there was to know, but never spoke of who he was.

Lancelot had returned almost every year. This time, too, he regained his sense of balance. The sun had sunk low in the sky when he took his leave.

"Once more you have given me strength, my dear friend," he said.

The old man looked at him gravely. Abruptly he gestured.

"Be on your guard against Sir Modred," he said.

"Sir Modred?" Lancelot asked in surprise. "But why?"

"He plans in secret the overthrow of the Round Table."

"*Sir Modred?* The King's wife's brother?"

The old man nodded. "He will break faith," he said. Then he turned on his heel and went back into his hut.

Sir Lancelot mounted. For once he could not bring himself to believe what the holy man had said.

Merlin heard the thud of the horse's hooves die away in the stillness of the woods. His heart was filled with sadness. He thought of Sir Lancelot who, more than any of the other knights, had come to stand for the principles of the Order. Again and again he defended the oppressed, helped the poor. But he was unable to help himself.

Merlin sighed. He took down his record of the reign

and laid it open on the table. He pulled up a chair and began to write:

At this time King Arthur had reigned for almost ten years. He had been a light-bringer: a king who brought his people to the knowledge of God. In these ten years the rule of force had been replaced by more humane laws; churches and monasteries had been founded, new roadways had been laid; peace set on secure footings. Sir Lancelot too was a light-bringer, a man who worked unceasingly to fulfil the King's commands, although his love for Guinevere was consuming his heart. Sir Welwyn and Sir Cynric, Sir Pellinore, Balin and Balan rode out against injustice and oppression.

Guinevere the Queen had a quiet and steadfast will. She sat at the King's side; her strength upheld him. Never a soft and easy creature, she held to her purpose, driving the King on the road that turns a man inward to know the country of his own heart and mind: to teach him to know himself: to teach him to be perfect.

There were many who understood the greatness of King Arthur's struggle to establish his ideal and who came to his Hall to offer their services and to sit at the Round Table, where all were welcome. But many others failed to grasp the King's high purpose. Sir Modred did not understand it, nor did the Lord of Brodeshead, nor many others. In their blindness these men felt that King Arthur's humanity darkened their honour. They formed a secret and shameful alliance. I warned the King, but Arthur still could not comprehend the power his brother-in-law held, and the terrible purpose for which he had gathered it.

So the hosts of light and the hosts of darkness confronted one another, ready at the stirrup for the clash.

Sir Modred was sitting by the open fire with the Lord of Brodeshead. He had won his host's full support. Brodeshead had had enough of the skyfoot dreamer who sat in the King's Seat. He would pretend to leave his tenant farmers in peace, for the moment. But the secret plans were ready.

Brodeshead's daughters served the men cups of beer. "Your two girls are beautiful," Modred remarked to his host. "Have no lords come to ask for them in marriage?"

Brodeshead bent forward and whispered: "Beautiful they may be, but they are wildcats with it, though a man should not say such a thing of his daughters."

Sir Modred laughed. And suddenly he was struck by an outrageous idea. He looked at the lord's beautiful daughters. Could he not exploit them, as a forger makes use of false coin!

"Wildcats have their uses," he said lightly. Then he leaned forward and told Brodeshead his plan. He spoke of Balin and Balan, who were among the bravest knights of the Round Table.

"They are silent men. Each dreams of displaying his courage in front of some lovely girl. They long for love, but they are stiff blunt men, and women mock them for it."

"And you think that my daughters—?" Brodeshead looked questioningly at Modred.

"This will be our first blow for the kingship. Listen carefully!"

The flames licked round the logs in the open hearth as Sir Modred set out his plan to the Lord of Brodeshead.

10

Balin and Balan

King Arthur sat in the Great Hall of Camelot with a number of the Round Table knights. Welwyn, newly back from a great journey, was telling his adventures; his hearth-companions were listening, fascinated, to his descriptions of a duel fought at owl-light, in the ghost-time of the day. It had been a long fight and a fierce one, until at last, abruptly, the unknown challenger had swung his horse round and ridden off into the dark.

"Wherever I rode men knew the names of the knights of the Round Table," he said. His voice was gay and pleased. "Everywhere I went boys came begging to serve as my squire!"

Balin leaned forward. He had been staring at a withered rose hanging from Welwyn's belt. He imagined some lovely girl handing it to Welwyn.

"Tell us about the flower!" he said brusquely.

"This rose?" Welwyn laughed. "A girl gave it to me—a pretty sweet-tempered child." He described willingly, eagerly, how he had won the girl's heart.

Balin leaned forward again. "What was she like?" The tone of his voice made Welwyn realize for the first time how much Balin longed for a woman to love him.

He chose his words carefully and spoke in a quiet voice.

"All women have eyes—hers were brown. All women have lips; hers were red. All women have hair, and hers was fair. All women seek a man, Balin, and she sought me!" He gave his friend a nod of encouragement and picked up his tankard.

At that moment a servant entered and whispered something in King Arthur's ear.

"A lady? At this late hour? Let her come in."

Welwyn had put his tankard down again. The whole company turned to look towards the door. The servant brought in a girl. She was slender. A kerchief was tied over her head, but her face was uncovered, and they saw that she had great beauty. She curtsied to the king.

"What brings you here, lady? Who are you?"

"My name is Enid, my lord the High King. I am mistress of the lands and steading of Stamford Ridge. A month ago a warrior lord came, strong as a bear, dressed all in the colour of saffron. He is as clever as a fox, as sly-striking as a snake. He seized my Hall and made himself master of my lands. Now he is demanding my hand as well."

She hung her head. "Swallow a tear now and then," Sir Modred had told her; and her father, the Lord of Brodeshead, had added, "No man can hold out against the sight of a lovely girl in tears." She drew a long sighing breath.

"Was there no man to take up arms in your defence?" Welwyn exclaimed indignantly.

"Four lords had compassion on me. Each rode out for me in turn. All four were defeated!" Again she swallowed tears. "I slipped away from the Hall at night and rode to your court, my lord King. No woman appeals in vain to the Knights of the Round Table."

Balin was on his feet. Welwyn's words about the rose still rang in his head and, in some strange way, gave him confidence. Had he not said that every girl sought a man?

The other knights stared in surprise.

"My lord the High King, allow me to set right this wrong!"

King Arthur looked at Balin. He saw the amazement in Balan's face. In the short silence that followed, Balin would not look up. He grew unsure of himself; he became hesitant. What use would this lovely girl have for a graceless creature like him?

King Arthur rose. He saw Balin's hesitation and because of this wanted all the more to lay this charge on him. "My Lady of Stamford Ridge, one of my bravest and most loyal knights will champion you. Balin rates himself low, but we rate him exceeding high, and he will stand boldly in your name; he will serve you as a true man and ride gladly out to fight in your defence."

The girl sank in a curtsey. She bit back a smile. The affair was shaping as Sir Modred had said it would do.

The following morning Balin rode out with the girl. The sight of him, awkward at her side, was a touching one. He was dreaming of a cherished hope fulfilled: himself defeating the mighty lord in saffron yellow and winning this lovely girl to be his love.

On the following day Arthur sat in the King's Seat and held his court. As usual, a stream of people had come to hear him give his judgments. Now a young man, little more than a boy, came forward. He carried himself proudly. His confident gaze held firm on Arthur the King. He knelt at the king's knee.

"My lord the High King," he said, "my name is Bedivere. My father's lands are small and our steading a poor one. I have left my father's Hall to come and serve you. I beg you to take me as your shield-bearer. Let me carry out your orders. Let me earn sword and shield, hauberk and helm. Let me win the name of knight."

King Arthur smiled. He liked the look of this boy. The way that he and so many others of his age came to Camelot, drawn there by tales they had heard about the Knights of the Round Table, warmed his heart. Some men belittled the Order, others debased its symbols, but boys like these saw and recognized their shining.

"You offer to be my servant, Bedivere. Do you know what service means?"

"I will serve you, King Arthur!"

"To serve a lord is to act as he bids you, in obedience to his commands."

"Let me serve you and obey you until I die!" said Bedivere. His voice had the plain directness of youth. He had a great deal to learn.

"I accept your service and your obedience gladly," the King said. He turned to one of the squires. "Find Bedivere quarters and take him to Sir Kay."

"Sir Kay . . .?" Bedivere stared in disappointment at the King. "It was you that I came to serve."

The King smiled. Youngsters came to his court longing to win fame and honour. They saw themselves riding out in bright mail, to conquer in the name of some righteous cause. How could they understand that the first thing a king needed was loyal and obedient service?

"Sir Kay is under obedience to me. I am his lord, he is my man," said the King. "He who serves Sir Kay, Bedivere, serves me."

Bedivere bowed. He turned to follow the squire. He had never heard of Sir Kay: still, here he was, under the King's roof-tree, among his hearth-companions. He would see the Knights of the Round Table: Lancelot, Welwyn, and the rest. And one day, surely, he too would be high among the lords of the King's House.

The King's next plaintiff was a young girl, a lord's daughter. Her eyes were downcast. She stood there before the King's Seat, helpless and despairing. Her voice seemed to die away as she described how her sick father had fallen into the power of his armourer, a man whom many men feared.

"He is oppressing our people. They are in misery." She let her voice sink. "He has forced me to give him my promise of marriage—I cannot repeat the means he used . . ." Her voice was choked with tears. "Be sure to cry well," Modred had said. Brodeshead's younger daughter stole a glance at the lords of Arthur's Hall. She saw she could fool all these famous knights.

Balan was on his feet. He came forward to the King's Seat. That same morning he had watched his brother ride out with a lovely girl at his side.

"My lord the High King," he said, and was startled by his own voice, "let me serve this lady!"

She looked at him in disdain. He was plain, short, thick-set. "Only the strongest of men could defeat the armourer," she said softly.

King Arthur saw Balan hesitate. He too was being rated low by a woman; but he too, like his brother, must overcome the awkwardness that troubled him in women's company.

"I grant the request," said the King. He turned to the lady. "Balan will serve you faithfully. He will stand up boldly in your name."

Balan left the King's Hall. He armed himself, saddled his horse, and rode out behind the Lady of Riversrow. And only then did he understand how his brother had felt. He too was dreaming: he dreamt of defeating the armourer, and of being accepted as his lady's knight.

And so Balin and Balan rode out. In the great woods

of the north where they were raised, they had learnt to take life as it came. They were plain men, and innocent. They did not see that they were like chessmen, moved on a board, in a game of the devil's making.

Merlin spurred his horse onward. Would he come in time, or was the hour already past and gone? That afternoon he had heard that Balin and Balan had ridden out, each in the service of a lord's young daughter. For a moment he had been surprised; then, knowing, as he did, the hearts of men, he realized what had happened. Sir Modred had ridden to Brodeshead. And Brodeshead had two daughters. Modred had strung his first trap to mesh and destroy the Knights of the Round Table.

Merlin rode on through the night-hours. He had meant to hold himself apart from the struggles of Arthur's reign, but this time his indignation had overcome him. He had buckled his sword belt, put on his pilgrim's cloak, and, borrowing a horse from Hector, had ridden out at full speed. His thoughts were with Balin and Balan. They were going to a terrible end—

Abruptly, without warning, the horse stumbled. Merlin had difficulty in keeping his seat. He wanted to ride on, but the animal was trembling. Merlin dismounted quickly. The horse gave a plaintive whinny, and then sank to the ground.

The moonshine whitened the fields. Merlin knelt at the horse's side. The animal gazed at him helplessly. Then its eyes filmed over. Its shivering and shaking were stilled.

Powerless, Merlin gazed round. He could not now reach journey's end in time. Must Balin and Balan ride out to their deaths?

The night spread out around him. The sky flickered with stars: behind those he saw were others, and behind those yet more, an infinity of stars. And beyond that infinity, other stars perhaps, other planets; eternity beyond man's imagining.

Merlin felt his anger sink. He saw the smallness of his powers. And he saw, more clearly than he had ever seen, that he could not shape what happened as he chose. He could not save Balin and Balan. Standing there, under a sky thick with stars, he saw that he must accept their deaths.

The girl took Balan to a Hall far from Camelot. She showed him a bed standing in a bare room. Hauberk, shirt and hose lay ready for him, stained yellow with saffron. The light was dim; Balan did not notice the colour. He was looking only at the girl.

"Tomorrow you will show yourself my true knight, my lord!" she said. "Rest now. I will come to your door tomorrow at first light. Wear the gear I have set ready— it is finer than your own, and I chose it, my lord, for you. Here is a helmet, with a visor to cover and protect your face."

She came closer. He smelt the sweetness of her hair.

"I have brought you a token, my lord Balan. Pin my rose over your heart."

Balan took the rose and thanked her. "I will fight for

you," he said. For her sake he would ride out gladly,
were it the Devil himself who came.

The Lady of Stamford had taken Balin to a small
deserted steading. "Rest now, Balin. Soon you will show
yourself my true knight!"

She slipped off her glove, kissed it and handed it to
Balin. "Wear my glove on your shield tomorrow!"

He, too, was given new armour and a helmet to cover
and protect his face; it was made after the eastern
pattern. He wore it when the lady came for him early on
the following morning.

"I shall fight for you," he said, as he stood ready to
ride out.

"Do you see the Hall that lies against the sun?" She
pointed. "He will come riding out through that gate:
a warlord all in saffron colour. Kill him for my sake!"

And so Balin and Balan, neither knowing who the
other was, rode out to meet in the early morning. Each
rode with a singing heart. Each had given his word and
was true to it.

"I shall fight for her, so help me God!" Balin looked
at the glove on his shield and rode forward at the gallop.

"I shall save my lady, so help me God!" Balan
fastened the rose on his breast, and he too spurred his
horse to the gallop.

The first clash was horrifying. Both lances shattered.
The horses reared and screamed. As the first shock died
away, Balin and Balan each realized his opponent's
strength. Only one man would ride alive from this fight.
They struck savagely at one another.

Hours passed. The horses were exhausted. Their
halters were curdled with foam. Balin and Balan dismounted and fought on. Blood seeped through their
hauberks, staining the bright mail. Even the rose was
dark with blood. Sweat streamed down under the

armour. Balin struggled to lift his sword: after hours of fighting, it was like lead in his hands, yet he brought it swinging down again, striking at his adversary—and as he brought up his dented shield to take the blow, his knees buckled and he almost fell. There was a chance, a moment; but Balin lacked the strength to raise his sword again; he could barely keep his feet. He thought of the girl's eyes; the memory helped him to stand his ground.

Now Balan raised his sword, slowly, gripping both hands about the hilt. This must be the death blow. If it failed he was lost. The girl's voice echoed in his ears. Her whispered words kept him on his feet. He gathered the last of his strength and swung his great sword slowly upward. Down it came; it thundered on his opponent's shield and glanced along the shoulder-blade, where the hauberk was torn and buckled. The force of his own blow brought Balan to his knees.

The knight in yellow was on his knees, but Balin could hardly see him, for he was blinded by blood, and the broad nose-piece of his helmet, dented by an earlier blow, blocked his field of sight. Gasping for breath, leaning on his sword, he took a step forward; he had to move cautiously, fearing that he might collapse with the shifting of his own weight. He tried to lift his sword. Was the sword-blade trapped? Had his opponent gripped hold of it? The world drifted and scattered before his eyes. Through a haze he saw the knight in yellow struggle to rise and fail to lift himself from his knees.

The fight had gone on for hours. Balin staggered: he could not lift his sword. He thought of the lady, but even her image could not help him now. Slowly he loosed his grip on his sword. He sank on one knee for support, but the knee could not bear his weight and he fell forward. Where was Balan, his brother? Far away in the King's Hall—He heard three blasts ring out on a distant hunting horn. Was the hunt over? Had the kill been made?

Balan was trying to rise, unaware that his opponent had collapsed at his side. He shivered. His fingers touched the bloody rose on his breast. Sweat ran under his battered armour. The armourer was unbelievably strong.

Balan struggled to rise. Where was his sword? He must defeat the armourer; he must free the girl. And after that? Leaning on one knee, with blood and sweat blinding his eyes, Balan groped for his sword. He willed himself to stand, but he could not do it: he fell and lay still as stone. For a moment all was silent and dark. He realised that his heart-beat was fading. From a long way off he heard a voice say: "Tell me your name, sir!"

"My name is Balan, sir. My brother is the great Balin." His head felt light now, as if the blood had drained away, and the pain with it. He was as light as air and perfectly calm.

"Balan! Balan, I am . . . Balin!" The voice seemed to break. For the last time Balan tensed his muscles, gathered his strength, and stretched out one hand; and Balin too made a last effort and reached out. With a clink of metal the mailed hands touched.

"I was fighting for a lady."

"I, too, was fighting for a lady."

"Was she beautiful?"

"Yes, she was beautiful."

"Describe her."

They did not see that the two girls had come forward to bend over them; nor did they notice Sir Modred, watching with satisfaction from the trees.

"She sought a man to stand for her. She chose me."

Balan smiled, but his mouth was hidden by the battered helmet.

"My girl was like sunlight in a clearing among the trees. Listen, Balan; she was like—"

Balan was listening, but he could no longer hear his dying brother's voice.

"Listen, Balin," he whispered in his turn. "My hands are like hide, but her touch softened them. Listen—"

The place where they had fought was silent. Sprawled in the dust, Balin and Balan had stretched out their hands to each other. The world shrank smaller and smaller as they lay there, but the bright air spread out all about them. Everything was quiet. Only the lips under the dented helmets still moved, shaping words no man could hear, to speak of a girl like sunlight in a clearing, and the freshness of morning springing out across the world.

"Dear God," one said, quiet and at rest.

"Aye, dear God."

The women looked at one another. They saw the bloody glove pinned to the shield, the bloody rose in the gaping armour. They realized too late what manner of men they had destroyed.

Late that night they knocked at a convent door. The abbess never knew why these two girls, high-born and beautiful, chose to renounce the world and turn to God. From time to time she heard them mention two names: Balin and Balan. But she had never heard of the men who served Arthur the King. The convent was a place shut away from the world; for her the names had no meaning.

II

The Making of a Man

Guinevere put her hand on King Arthur's arm as if by doing so she could strengthen him. They were alone together. They had talked for a long time: about their marriage, about the Round Table, about the kingdom. But all their talking had come to little. She could not lift the King's sadness. The deaths of Balin and Balan had shocked him deeply. He had ordered that a great search be mounted, but it had been in vain. The two girls who had come to Camelot had disappeared without trace.

Balin and Balan were dead. "I should never have let them go. They trusted me with their lives!" King Arthur had said. Self-reproach lay heavily on him. He saw how separate were the world he dreamed of and the world he walked in. He had wanted to channel his life like water flowing in a river, but now he felt drained, empty, dry. Guinevere closed her hand tighter on his arm.

King Arthur looked at her. "All this has made me so tired," he said. Guinevere rose and went to the door.

"Call Guy to the King," she told a servant. The pressures of life in the King's House had borne on her too long and too sharply. There was always anxiety, worry about campaigns, uncertainty about conditions in the kingdom. In a little while the King must go down to meet with the Knights of the Round Table. He must seem to be untroubled; his strength of mind and will

96

must be as firm as ever. He could never afford to seem heart-sick.

There was a knock at the door. Guy entered. He glanced quickly from one to the other to guess their mood. The Queen looked tired and sad. The King was sombre. He thought it a miracle that they had not collapsed under the great disappointments of their life.

"Death must have his harvest home, like any other reaper," Guy said, looking at the King.

"This harvest was a bad one."

"Even after a bad harvest, my lord King, one must go out and sow. As a man sows, so shall he reap, my lord the High King. The world is hungry for the fruits of the earth."

The King closed his eyes, as if trying to imagine the harvest of all his efforts for Britain. "I know that the world is hungry and crying out. But the fruits of my patch of earth are greed, power, and vain-glory!"

"My lord the High King," Guy said seriously, "thistles and poppies flower in the corn, but the grain still grows. I have come to value life in spite of its disappointments. Send your knights out across your land to judge its harvest. Perhaps they will find the answers to your questions. A man must go out into the dark to see the stars, my lord."

Guy saw that his words had moved the King.

King Arthur found himself remembering the tales he had heard as a boy. Men said that he who held the Grail had in his hands the secret of life. Should he send his knights out in search of the Grail? Here perhaps might be a solution to the cares of the kingdom.

Sir Modred glanced round the small circle. A great fire blazed up brightly on the hearth. The flickering light of torches washed the Hall of Alton Priors. The draughts were icy; Modred, however, felt his triumph warm him. Once again he had carried out a double mission. The lord of Alton Priors and his men would be formidable allies.

"In a few years I shall be ready," said Modred. "When the time is ripe for the battle, I will send my signal."

"Why not strike sooner?" The lord of Alton Priors was impatient for plunder.

"Arthur has a great force at his back," said Modred. "I choose to wait until I am absolutely sure that I can strike and win."

He was a man for patient waiting, this Sir Modred: a chess player who paused to consider each move, and whose tactics were those of a great master of the game.

From Alton Priors Modred rode to Lord Ither's Hall, to reprimand him in the King's name.

Lord Ither was, he knew, an embittered man. Such men were capable of reckless action—particularly a man made as Ither was made, standing head and shoulders above his fellows, known and feared for his great strength.

"But neither my strength nor my courage stand to my advantage now," Ither said to Modred, angily thumping the table-board. Hairs bristled across his knuckles. "The land lies at peace. These days men no longer draw sword to settle their grievances; instead they sit down and prattle at the peace-makers' table. I have had plenty of chances to enlarge my lands, but again and again the King sends messengers to check me. Who do they think I am? A saint? Can a man no longer live like a man?"

Modred leaned forward. "There are some who think that way, but not I!"

"You have come to my Hall in the King's name. What do I care for a king who thinks my strength and my courage valueless? He even refused to name me a Knight of the Round Table!"

The game was as good as won, Modred thought with satisfaction. Just by listening, by watching for a man's weakness, he strengthened his position with every move he made.

Ither was a chieftain made after the old pattern: he knew only one way of life—that of the sword. He found satisfaction in fighting: for cattle, for pasture, for fishing rights, for women. And there were other men like him in the land of Britain. King Arthur was a fool who went against the current of his time. "Listen carefully, Lord Ither, I have a plan."

Ither listened. Pleasure began to spread across his stern face. This Modred had the devil's wits.

"Lancelot is on a mission to Rome," Modred said, when he had explained his plan. "Welwyn has been sent as Arthur's envoy to the King of the Scots. Balin and Balan are dead. Which of the Knights of the Round Table would dare to measure his strength against yours, Lord Ither?" Modred drank to his host. "Come to the King's Hall on the Friday before the feast of St. Denis and do as I have told you!"

"I shall come harnessed in scarlet!"

With a great gathering of his knights about him, Arthur the King held court. It was the Friday before the feast of St. Denis. As usual, people had come from far and wide to kneel at the King's Judgement Seat. They came with requests. They came to ask for support.

Sometimes they came to beg for help. Many of their problems made the King despair: he felt himself powerless to lighten his people's lives. The darkness in his kingdom was implanted too deep for his uprooting.

Once more the doors were opened. A lord came striding in, blazing in red hauberk and helmet, red shirt, red hose. He towered head and shoulders above the King's guard. Every man and woman in the Hall was staring at him, and he knew it and was glad of it. There was defiance in every line of him.

The lord stood before the King's Seat. He bowed briefly.

"My name is Ither. They call me the Terrible," he said. His words dropped heavily into the silence. "I have come, my lord, to appeal to the High King of this kingdom."

"Speak freely, Lord Ither," the King said. He knew this was no ordinary coming.

Ither drew himself up to his full height. "There was a time when I carried my sword for this kingdom. There was a time when I could toss down my strength as the stake, and by right of it have and hold what I won. There was a time when a man could act like a man. Those days, High King, are gone!"

King Arthur knew that all men were watching him. He knew too what lay behind Ither's words. It was vital that he found the right answer.

"What makes a man, Lord Ither? The strength of his sword? His hand's skill and cunning? Or something more?" He leaned forward. "A man is more than brute strength. He has a heart and a mind, a conscience, a sense of duty. It is these that make a man!"

The people watched and listened, enthralled. The two men were meeting in single combat, armed with words in place of weapons. They had run the first list; neither stood out as winner.

"Milky words like these do not make a man, High

King. You under-estimate the realities of life. The people are using us, the lords of this land, like pieces in a game; and the prize they play for, my lord King, is private gain. I live, High King; I hold my lands; no man shall take what is mine. I appeal to you, the High King of this kingdom: set a new course. Men are men, not saints— they do not care for their fellows' well-being, they will not make ready sacrifices! The King stands now for new ways, new beliefs, and the strength of his kingdom is undermined."

Spellbound by his words, the King's knights stared at Arthur. A whispering spread through the Hall.

My answer will be of immense importance, thought King Arthur. The past came riding here against the present—a past as old as the hills, but a newcomer to the King's Hall.

"Am I to believe in the goodness of men, when day after day I see their weakness?" Ither asked. The words sounded ironical and airy, but as the King answered, his voice was suddenly stronger, and it was plain that he was holding back anger.

"A man's love for his fellows is what makes him a man, Ither! At my crowning I swore that my people should have justice. Now, as then, I mean to rule by justice, not by the sword."

The red lord took a step forward. "Try to make the King lose his temper in the end," Sir Modred had told him.

"Time out of mind the lords of this kingdom passed judgment in their own lands. A lordless man was ill-cared for then, High King, for he had none to fight for him. Men should live the way of life to which they are called: the poor in poverty, the farmer growing food, the priests praying to God. And the lords, High King, from time immemorial have been put on this earth to carry arms!"

"And to destroy in one day what the farmer has

laboured for year-long!" King Arthur had sprung to his feet.

"High King," said Ither, encouraged to see the King's anger, "you over-estimate the people. They want to live and die in peaceful stupidity. It takes a fool, lord King, to reward stupidity with justice."

King Arthur had sat down again. He knew that he should not have shown anger.

"That will do," he said. He spoke calmly but his voice was sharp. "We thank you for your concern for the welfare of this kingdom. We do not doubt your strength and courage—only your convictions. When you go out from this my Hall, Lord Ither, set your mind to consider whether or not wisdom is superior to force."

The irony in the King's voice had its effect. Now it was Ither's anger which flared up. The King's knights nudged one another.

"High King," Ither said grimly, "if there is one knight in your Hall who wants to prove himself a man, let him stand forward and challenge me to single combat."

For a moment silence fell on the Hall. Ither began to laugh scornfully.

"You see, Arthur the King! Wisdom is just a fine-sounding word. You keep cowards at your hearth."

"Come, Lord Ither, calm yourself," Sir Modred exclaimed, with pretended indignation.

The King looked at his wife's brother in thanks.

But Ither drew his sword and said, "If any one among you is man enough to meet with me in combat, he will find me on the wood-shore. I will wait until the going down of the sun."

As Ither left the Hall, Sir Cynric, the young Bedivere, Sir Owen, Gawain, Kay, indeed nearly all the Knights of the Round Table sprang forward. Each of them pledged himself to defend the Order's honour against Lord Ither. The King thanked them, but he would not accept any man's offer to stand for him. In spite of their protests, he had his horse saddled and put on his armour.

Modred came to him. "You must not set the kingship in danger because of a braggart like Ither," he said seriously. "Let me ride out in your stead."

King Arthur shook his head, though he thanked him.

"What do you hope to prove by meeting this man in single combat?" Guinevere asked. "The only men who need to prove themselves are those who are irresolute and uncertain."

"I must show the people that my beliefs are not rooted in cowardice. You heard Ither's words. If I ignored his challenge, I would lose my authority. I beg you to understand."

But Guinevere refused to understand, and King Arthur rode out with a heavy heart to prove by force of arms that wisdom was a better thing than force. Life was a strange and contradictory business.

He came to the wood-shore, but Lord Ither was not there. He found fresh traces of horses' hooves in the trodden moss. Someone had been before him: some unknown knight had seized the chance of combat. Arthur waited. But no one came. His hope of proving his courage was snatched away: he was too late. Some

wandering knight had challenged Ither, struck him down, and carried the wounded man to his Hall at his saddle-bow, then ridden on to new encounters. Arthur waited still as the sun sank and owl-light spread across the wood-shore: a lonely and disappointed man.

103

Late that night the King sat alone in a small room behind the Hall, staring into the fire that burned on the hearth-stone. His marriage to Guinevere was a difficult one. She had sharply condemned the Order's quest for the Holy Grail.

"You have no right to send out your knights to seek something that cannot be found," she had told him. "What are you seeking? Greater fame? Greater honour? Do you want to be wiser than life itself?"

"You do not understand."

"I neither want to understand this nor can I do so."

King Arthur stared unhappily into the fire. What had he accomplished with all his striving to create a peaceful kingdom? The Knights of the Round Table had ridden out in search of the Holy Grail. Many of them had returned with marvellous tales to tell. But the Grail still lay hidden. Was Guinevere right after all? Should he put an end to their seeking?

He could not sit any longer companied by his unhappiness. He called for Guy.

"What is fame, Guy?"

Guy looked at the King. He saw how tired and sombre he looked as he sat there by the fire.

"Fame is relative, always relative, so much so that a man can never hold it in his hand. Yet it bears no relation to the effort a man must make to win it."

"What makes you say that, Guy?"

For a moment Guy's eyes were grave. His face bore no flicker of his usual airy mockery.

"Because I value your fame, my lord the High King. I know that your efforts have been unceasing."

"Thank you," the King said. "I am grateful." He looked into the fire, where the last log was crumbling into ash. The fire had glowed brightly and had warmed him as he sat there. Now only a handful of ashes remained. If fame fell away like ash, what was it that made a man into a man?

12

The Great Game

Sir Modred drained his cup and watched Lancelot, who sat nearly opposite him on the far side of the table. A servant was bringing round pasties. Lancelot was looking at the Queen. The unguarded look showed clearly how much he loved and honoured her. The truth flashed on Modred. He tried to hide his excitement. Lancelot was in love, in love with Guinevere.

There could be no doubt. Sir Modred stole a glance at the Queen. She sat quietly at the King's right hand, her eyes cast down. For a moment she glanced swiftly up at Lancelot, but immediately she dropped her eyes once more.

Guinevere knew that Lancelot loved her.

Thoughts raced through Modred's head. Any living man could be brought to doubt. One had only to pick the right words. Modred knew, better than any other man, how rumour could undermine a man and bring him down. There were already whispers about Arthur's marriage to Guinevere: men were saying it had proved a difficult one.

Lancelot and Guinevere: it was perfect for his purposes. He signed to a servant to refill his cup. He drank to the King, then lifted his cup to the Queen, and then, still holding the cup, he glanced casually at Lancelot.

"Lancelot, you are very quiet!" He spoke lightly and gaily. "Perhaps you are in love."

Modred noticed with satisfaction that King Arthur looked towards Lancelot as if surprised and pleased at the notion. Guinevere stared straight in front of her. It was too straight a stare. For a moment there was a painful silence. Lancelot was too frank to deny his love, yet he could not declare it openly. Modred laughed.

Lancelot leaned back in his chair and glanced round the circle. "Yes," he said, "I am in love!" He spoke lightly, as a man entering into a joke: "I am in love and I carry my heart on my sleeve."

Arthur the King stared at his wife's brother. "I cannot believe it," he whispered, sick at heart.

"My lord the High King," said Modred, "for a long time I hoped to keep it from you. But I cannot be silent when your household laughs and mocks you in secret."

"Are you telling me that men say openly that they are lovers?"

"Not openly, High King. Men whisper it. No one has dared to stand before your face and tell you the truth."

"It cannot be true," King Arthur said. But he spoke without certainty.

"You see now, lord King, why Lancelot rides away so often, and why your marriage has crumbled. It will not be difficult to prove that I speak the truth."

"Leave me now," said the King.

Sir Modred bowed. "I know what you are feeling," he said. "But I felt it my duty—"

"Very well. Now leave me."

Sir Modred withdrew, laughing to himself. He had been anxious about this conversation, but it had been so easy a child could have conducted it.

King Arthur sat alone with his doubts, watching the flames flicker on the hearth-stone. He heard Merlin's voice again, a long way off down the years.

Lancelot, Guinevere: was it this that had soured his marriage? Small details came into his mind: a word, a gesture, an expression. His doubts grew deeper and sharper. Should he dismiss Lancelot from his House? Send him on some impossible mission? Did his wife mean more to Lancelot than life itself?

Once the thought of Guinevere had made the world sing. Was happiness as brittle as Merlin had said? Had Merlin seen what would happen between him and Guinevere?

On an impulse the King went to the Queen's Room.

"Guinevere, what is it that has come between us?"

She looked at him, searching for words.

"Perhaps your high hopes have come between us." Her voice was a whisper. "You have given me my part in the glory and the shining of your kingship, but that was not what I dreamed of—You are trapped in the meshes of a task no man can fulfil. The Order's ideals are your only escape. The Arthur I married, he was his own man, but he has disappeared . . ." Her voice was dull and tired.

"What do you mean—disappeared? Explain what you mean!" In his helplessness he shouted the words.

Guinevere shrugged her shoulders wearily. "You have
taken too much on yourself. You are struggling to work
harder than any living man could do, for the sake of the
kingdom, and in the struggle you have lost yourself. You
have married yourself to your hopes. What kind of wife
can I be for such a man? You have done a great deal
for your kingdom and your people, more than I would
have thought possible. No one knows this better than I
do. But in doing it you have outgrown me, left me
behind—"

Arthur took Guinevere's hands in his. They were cold.
"Don't you see that I am lonely?"

Guinevere began to weep. "You cannot remake
yourself. And I cannot either." She drew her hands
away. The King despaired; he cried out angrily: "Do
you know why Lancelot keeps away from the King's
House?"

Guinevere was shaken. What made him ask such a
question? Did he not even trust her? She looked straight
at him. Her voice hardened.

"Yes," she said. "I know why."

For a moment King Arthur stood there. He looked at
his wife. Then he turned on his heel and left the room.

Standing in the doorway of his hut, Merlin watched
the clouds. It was the hour of the sun's going down, and
the air was streaked with gold. He went back into the
hut, took down the parchment and wrote in his careful,
clear script:

*Arthur hoped to spend the small space of his life bringing
light into his kingdom. The task was too great for any living
man. In his efforts he grew away from his wife, and came to
stand completely alone. He longed for a tranquil and gentle life,
but he could not give up his image of knighthood. Down all the
years to come, men will reach out for the image of Arthur's
making. But Sir Modred's plans have changed the King.
Something has died in him. He still sits among his knights of*

the Round Table, but his heart is there no longer. He hears pleas and gives judgment as he has always done, but his voice is tired. "It is the Queen's fault," the Knights say. "The King is grieving because the Queen loves Lancelot." Sadness is spreading through the King's House and men hold Queen Guinevere responsible.

One evening Sir Modred took Lancelot's arm and led him to a quiet niche in one of the passages.

He spoke quietly. His voice was affectionate and friendly: "The King's House is a sad place these days. I want to speak frankly. The King has discovered your love for the Queen."

Lancelot seized Modred's shoulders. "That is impossible. I have struggled all my life to keep it secret."

"No one knows that better than I do," Modred said. He shook his head. "The King is increasingly suspicious, and he holds you responsible. The other night he came to the Queen's Room. He was shouting, so they say. The Queen asks to have secret word with you."

Lancelot shook his head. It was impossible for him to go to the Queen.

"You *must* go, Lancelot, for the King's sake as well as the Queen's. She expects you in her room. Go there after midnight. Everything has been arranged. Your visit will be kept secret. The door will be unlocked. This is the message she sends you."

"But Modred—" Lancelot began. He was shocked and confused, and there were a hundred questions he wanted to ask. But someone was coming.

"You must go!" Modred whispered urgently.

"My lord King, I must speak with you," said Modred.
"I am tired, Modred. Can it wait till morning?"
Modred shook his head.
"What is it?" King Arthur looked at his wife's brother.

Modred leaned forward. He exulted as he thought of his plan: brilliant in its daring.

"High King, Lancelot means to go to the Queen again tonight!"

"Again?"

Modred nodded. The game was easy. He saw that from the King's face.

"In your own interest, as well as for the sake of the Queen and of the kingdom, we must prevent this meeting!"

King Arthur remembered the words of St. Paul. He had written that love covered all things, promised all things, endured all things. "I cannot force your sister to love me, Modred. What do you want me to do? Lie in wait like a jealous husband? Split Lancelot's skull?" The King's voice was dull.

"High King, the interests of the kingdom must come first. Whispered slanders are already undermining your authority. Men say that you are afraid of Lancelot; that Lancelot and the Queen plan to seize the kingship. Men will begin to gather into factions, High King, and that will mean the seeding of new feuds." Modred took a step forward and looked into Arthur's eyes. He wanted the King to think that he found it hard to be so frank. "High King," he said gently but urgently, "you and I can understand that this meeting springs from human longing. It might be possible for you, or for me, her brother, to forgive them. But you cannot expect your people to do the same."

For a moment there was complete silence in the King's Room. The King was worn to death.

"How could it come to this, Modred?"

"One should not under-estimate the power of gossip, High King." He spoke gently but his heart was exhilarated: he had mentioned the tactics he himself had used, and by doing so could turn aside any possible suspicion.

"I cannot allow the making of new feuds—" The King spoke wearily. He knew that he must sacrifice his pride for the unity of his house and his kingdom; he must discover what lay between his wife and Lancelot.

Modred bowed. He acted as if he shared the King's sorrow and loneliness.

"Brother, will you do whatever must be done? I cannot bring myself to do it—But for the sake of the kingdom it must be so."

"Aye, my lord King," said Modred. He bowed gravely and withdrew. How easy it was to move the pieces in this game. In his mind's eye he surveyed the board he played on: the Knight would be taken, the Queen would be in check, the King was already seriously threatened.

It had all been so easy. He had bribed servants. He had won allies with fine promises. And when he dealt with men who could not be bought, he spread suspicion and doubt instead. Modred surveyed the game with pleasure. His position was a strong one.

Lancelot pressed his hands against his temples. Should he go to Guinevere, as Modred had advised? Should he go to the King and tell him that the tale was madness? The guard at the gate had been changed: he could ride out to forget in some far corner of the world. But what of Guinevere?

Sir Lancelot stood up. He would go to the Queen. Perhaps she could find some solution. He slipped quietly along the passages. No one challenged him. Cautiously he opened the door of the Queen's Room and closed it behind him without a sound. The room was dark. A single small torch was burning, its light a flicker on the wall. Someone was standing at the window.

"Is that you, Arthur?"

Dear God, thought Lancelot, bewildered. Was it not he she waited for? She had turned and was kindling a second torch.

"Lancelot!" Her voice shook with terror.

At that moment he heard someone in the passage.

Arms clashed; there was a clamour of voices and then a knocking at the door.

"Open the door," someone shouted: Gareth, his hearth-companion. He thought he heard Modred's voice too out there in the passage.

Guinevere stared at him. His eyes were bewildered. He stood alone, realizing too late that he was trapped.

"Come out, Lancelot!" someone called. Was it Kay's voice?

Lancelot turned to the Queen. "It is a trap," he whispered. "Modred said you must have speech with me."

Now she too realized their danger. Was there no escape?

The knocking at the door grew louder.

"We will open the door and go to the King," said Guinevere. "Our word will stand against Modred's."

"We could rely on nothing but our word alone—and my coming here puts proof in Modred's hand."

"Open the door!"

Lancelot looked round. There were no weapons in the room. He took up the iron poker. Guinevere shook her head. Her eyes stared like those of a dead woman. Lancelot went to her.

"They will kill me," he said quietly. "I am not afraid of death, but if I die no man alive will believe you innocent. For your sake I must live and hope to convince the King."

They were chopping at the door with an axe. The panels splintered.

"Come out, Lancelot! Come out like a man. Show yourself!"

Lancelot caught Guinevere's hands. "I mean to show myself at last," he said. He spoke urgently. "That day by the brook, when I was bringing you to the King's House, I went down into darkness for love of you, and have lived there ever since. Had you been promised to any other man, I would have carried you off at my saddle-bow. But I was Arthur's man and he was my friend above all others—"

The great axe crashed again through the door; it was giving way fast. There was little time left. "For your sake and for his I have to go on living: I will escape, Guinevere, and I will do all I can to put an end to this slander!" He crossed to the torches and doused them. "God be with you, Guinevere. Do not condemn my love. It is the best thing in me."

With the fire-iron in one hand, he drew back the door-bolt. Sir Pinel was first across the threshold, and a single blow brought him down. In the same instant Lancelot seized Pinel's sword and fought his way through the door, striking out to right and left. He struck hard, to kill. In the heat of the battle he heard Modred's voice, and rage doubled his courage. He hacked his way blindly through his hearth-companions, too angry and too desperate to know whom he struck in the flaring torch-lit darkness. Gaheris fell dying. Gareth was struck down. Gawain was wounded.

But other voices cried out down the passage and other men came running.

"Lancelot, stand firm!"

The enemy fell back. Lancelot's face ran with blood and sweat and tears. He saw Modred take to his heels, dragging away the wounded Gawain. A score of lords came running up, headed by Lancelot's cousin, Sir Bors, Eric de Maris and Lionel, all with drawn swords.

"Thank God, we are in time," said Bors. He drew Lancelot away. "Our horses are ready. Hurry, before it is too late!"

They hurried him along. They set him on his horse. A friend's hand gripped his rein, urging the horse forward at the gallop through the King's Gate.

They rode on through the dark night-hours. Not until first light, when at last they felt safe, did they stop to rest. Only then did Lancelot come to himself. His face was desolate.

"It will turn to good yet," Bors said with conviction. But Lancelot shook his head.

"It was not my choosing, but I was the King's man. I have broken the oath I swore at his knee, with my hands between his hands. I would have given my life for my hearth-companions, but I have sent them to their deaths. I wanted to spare the King and the Queen sorrow. And now—" He gazed at his friends in despair. "How was it possible for Modred to trap me like this?"

"Modred?" Bors exclaimed in surprise. "But it was Modred who warned me that you were in danger. It is thanks to Modred that we were able to reach you in time!"

"Dear God!" Lancelot was lost. He hid his face in his hands. The world fled away. Sir Bors caught him as he fell, and unbuckled his hauberk. Only then did he see the wounds.

114

13

The Investigation

"Lord Arthur, you *must* investigate this matter," said Modred. He deliberately did not use the King's title in order to lay stress on his own close relationship with him.

"I know it. I had already decided that I must hunt down the cause and lay it bare in the full light of noon. Let every man of my household stand ready tomorrow. If need be, I will not leave one stone of these walls standing upon another. Send out riders, Modred; let them summon Lancelot to judgment. Give him my word that nothing will befall him. I swear that he shall come in safety under my roof-tree and go again free from my gate. But I must know the truth."

A servant entered.

"What is it?"

"The Queen asks to speak with you, my lord the High King."

King Arthur shook his head. "Tell her that I am engaged on urgent matters."

The servant bowed and withdrew.

Arthur rose. "That is all," he said. "Tomorrow morning we will open the investigation."

Modred was amazed to see how quickly the King had recovered his old vitality. He could not understand the source of Arthur's strength of spirit. The King's face showed his determination; his will was set like iron. He was a man made to command; it was plain in every line of him.

"Modred." The King spoke in a quieter, milder voice. "I am not making this investigation for my own sake; nor even for the honour of my house. In a way what I am doing is done on Lancelot's behalf. I cannot believe that he has broken faith with me. Above all, it is done for the Queen. Whatever may have happened, she is my first concern."

"What do you hope to achieve?" asked Modred. The chess-pieces had been shifted unexpectedly; for a moment tactical control of the game slipped away from him.

"She is my wife and dear to me," the King said.

Modred nodded. He turned his face away from the King. His secret inner delight faded. The light-bringer's place on the board was stronger than he had realized. In making his moves, he thought he had taken everything possible into consideration: but he had under-estimated the strength of a man's love.

From his place in the corner of the King's Hall, Guy followed each move in the investigation. The crowd held its breath at the thrust and parry of question and answer. The King had summoned his whole household to the Hall. He sat alone in the Judgment Seat.

Guy listened to the Queen. "Sir Lancelot came to me after midnight. Sir Modred had told him that I wished to speak with him urgently."

"Is that true, Sir Modred?"

Modred rose from his seat. "It is quite true, High King. It was a servant, Owen, who asked me to deliver this message."

"Owen!" called the King. A brown-haired boy came forward.

"Did you give Sir Modred such a message?"

"Yes, my lord the High King," said Owen.

"Who told you to do so?"

"Sir Gaheris, High King," said Owen, without hesitation. A murmur of voices rose in the Hall. Sir Gaheris was dead. Guy looked at the Queen. She was white and looked worn to the bone.

The King called on Sir Gawain. "How did you know that Sir Lancelot was with the Queen?"

"Sir Pinel asked us to go at his side to the Queen's Room, High King," said Gawain. He drew himself up to his full height. "High King, I called Lancelot my friend. He has broken faith, brought the Queen's name into disrepute. And more than all this, he has murdered my brothers. I demand vengeance!"

His voice rang out through the Hall. There was a murmur of approval. Guy looked around him, gauging the mood of these assembled men. He found it difficult. Gawain was still the King's true man. But he was the Queen's man no longer; he was, it seemed, convinced of her guilt, although to spare the King he tried to conceal it.

Guy noticed that Welwyn looked bewildered. He had ridden out from Camelot many months earlier and had returned only the night before, to find the King's House turned to a place of mistrust and his hearth-companions full of suspicion.

"Sir Modred, what did Lancelot say when you gave him the message?"

Modred was silent for a moment. "He was taken aback, High King."

"And what else?"

"We talked for a long time," said Modred, as if he found it difficult to say the words. "I begged him to leave your House, High King. I tried to show him how spreading rumours undermined the kingship."

"What did he reply?" The King leaned forward, and Guy realized how much hung upon this answer.

"He said that he owed you loyalty. That he had acted as became both man and knight. That his love for the Queen lay hidden in his heart. That there was no disgrace in his love."

Guy saw the Queen look up in surprise. She had not expected these words. Would Modred stand as Lancelot's champion?

A number of lords were then called to explain why they had been outside the Queen's Room at the hour in question. One had fetched another, he a third, and so on. Modred, too, gave his account of what had happened.

"I was warned by Sir Gaheris. I heard the tumult in the passage. I begged the lords to leave, but they would not listen."

Again the Queen glanced at Modred in surprise. Guy held his breath as the swordplay of question and answer went on.

"And then?"

"Then I went to Sir Bors. I saw that great trouble would come of it, and I begged Bors, Sir Eric and several other knights to accompany me, and I went back with them to the passage outside the Queen's door."

A servant confirmed Modred's words.

"I urged Gawain to go with me, hoping that the others would follow, and this they did," said Modred.

He sat down, and the King nodded to him, a gesture of thanks. Of all the knights of the King's household, Modred had been the only one who had hoped to serve the King, the Queen and Lancelot, all three. Guy could not understand it. Had he been mistaken in Sir Modred?

Gawain had risen from his seat. He stepped forward.

"My lord the High King," he said, in a voice that shook with anger, "the only man who can answer all our questions is Lancelot. One word from him could have laid all suspicion to rest. But he has not come to stand in this Hall, and this alone proves his guilt. He killed my brothers, High King. I demand vengeance!"

Before Arthur could answer, the Queen rose to her feet. If Lancelot was guilty, so too was she. This was plain to everyone. For the sake of the King, as he sat alone in the

Judgment Seat, she now tried to find words with which
to come to her own defence.

"My lord King, when Lancelot came to my room that
evening, he spoke for the first time of his love for me. I
knew that he loved me, as any woman knows when a
man loves her. Nothing passed between us, then or at
any time, that could dishonour you, or him, or myself.
My lord, you know the hearts of men; do not condemn
the man who honoured and loved you above all others."

"He fought his way out from this House," the King
said. His voice was cold and hard.

"He fled this House that he might be free to prove his
innocence," said the Queen.

"Then why is he not here?"

"I claim that the ordeal of fire will prove I have spoken
the truth!" The Queen stood erect. Her words rang out.

A murmur of voices arose. Guy saw that the King was
profoundly shaken.

"High King, let me fetch Lancelot here!" cried
Gawain. "I will find him for you, if I must go down into
the underworld to do it."

Guy looked round. Was there no one who was clear-
sighted and calm enough to stem this flood of hatred?

Sir Welwyn stood forward. The Hall fell silent. "High
King," he said, "I have heard no word of mercy here
in this Hall. Any living man knows times of weakness,
but these do not make him a weakling. On the contrary,
it is the strength which enables him to realize and
conquer his weakness that makes him a man. If Lancelot
loved the Queen and his love drove him to undertake a
throng of dangerous tasks, if he has denied his dreams
and his longings because he is your loyal and loving
servant and because of that love for the Queen, then in
this there lies his making. This company condemns a
man for the merest flicker of weakness. Let me ride out,
High King, to call Lancelot to this Hall, so that a man

who is my friend and a great Knight of this Order, may stand safe before his hearth-companions."

The King's face softened a little. Guy felt the tension drop. Had Sir Welwyn's sense of mercy enabled him to find the needed words?

With his fellows and friends about him, Gawain again pressed forward. His voice was full of bitterness as he said: "That flicker of weakness, High King, cost Sir Pinel his life. It killed my brothers. Lancelot laid about him like a wild creature mad with rage. His life was safe in our hands, High King; we wished only to bring him before you. The verdict lies with you, my lord." He looked straight at the King. "An innocent man does not fight his way out, killing his hearth-companions to prove his own innocence! If the King calls treason and murder 'a moment of weakness', if in his mercy he condones such conduct, if he holds that lying and faithlessness are the making of a man—if you are such a king, my lord, I will live no longer in your Hall and stand no longer in your company."

The silence was absolute. Then Sir Welwyn sprang up again—but the Queen, too, had risen. She walked slowly forward to the King's Seat and looked up at him. Guy saw the glimmer of tears on her face, but her voice was quiet and steady.

"High King," she said, "Gawain grieves for his brothers and hates the man who killed them. So grieving, so hating, he accuses not Sir Lancelot alone, he also accuses me. What use are my words when men doubt me?" Guy held his breath as he watched the Queen's face. It was drained of colour, but she was still in great beauty. "I demand that God try me, High King. Only He can straighten this tangle of false-seeming and half-truth. I will have no man stand as my judge, but God only, committing my cause to Him, for He alone may see absolute truth. Let everything be ready within seven days. I demand trial by ordeal because I love you, my lord King, and honour all you have done as ruler of this kingdom."

Through her tears, Guinevere smiled at the King. Guy saw the King's sternness dissolve. His face was full of renewed love and trust; but clearly he knew, and suffered from the knowledge, how great a sacrifice the Queen made in her love for him. Unless God Himself spoke to save her from the fire, she would die in the flames to prove herself innocent.

King Arthur rose. For a moment it seemed as if even now he were looking for some other way. The Hall was as still as death.

"Let it be so. And may God be with us."

14

Trial by Ordeal

For three days and nights, Lancelot lay between life and death. Sir Bors, Sir Eric de Maris and the other knights watched over him by turns. They had built a lean-to shelter in the distant wood of Trenchiwain, and had cleaned and bandaged Lancelot's wounds. Now they took it in turns to sit beside him, keeping watch, for he was feverish and restless and every now and then would spring up as if trying to seize something that slipped from his grasp.

At last, however, he fell into a long and tranquil sleep. It was hours before he opened his eyes.

"Bors, where am I?"

"In the wood of Trenchiwain."

Lancelot's memory came slowly back. Alarmed and confused he asked what had happened that night at Camelot. "Gareth! Is Gareth dead?"

Bors nodded. "Go to sleep again," he said softly.

"And Gaheris? Is Gaheris dead?"

Bors nodded.

"They were my friends," said Lancelot. "I was mad with rage. I did not know at whom I struck."

"Go to sleep again," said Bors, but Lancelot shook his head.

"What will happen, Bors? What will the King think—and Guinevere? I must go back. What will they think of me if I do not?" He tried to get up, but Bors pushed him gently back onto the pallet.

"Who set this trap for me, Bors? If it was not Modred, who was it?"

"I don't know," said Bors. "Go to sleep, Lancelot."

All that day Lancelot lay there, without stirring, alone to question and wonder. He had let himself be used as a pawn; he had let himself be toppled into darkness. Whose fault was it? And what had happened to Guinevere?

"I have to go back to the King's House," Lancelot said on the evening of the fourth day.

"You must first recover your strength," said Eric de Maris.

"I must go to the King!" said Lancelot and sat up.

Sir Eric gently pushed him back.

"Later, Lancelot, when you have recovered."

In the deep woods of Trenchiwain, Lancelot and the twenty lords who were his loyal friends lived between hope and despair. And slowly, little by little, Lancelot recovered his strength.

On King Arthur's orders, Modred had sent out messengers to seek for Lancelot. He had chosen his own friends and allies for the task, and had given precise instructions for their ears only. Thus, on the afternoon of the fifth day, a rider came cantering into the distant wood of Trenchiwain. He thundered up to the doorway of the shack and swung himself off his foam-flecked horse.

"Where is Sir Lancelot?" he demanded, gasping for breath.

Sir Bors led him into the shelter. "Sir, I come from Camelot," said Modred's messenger. "In two days' time, Guinevere the Queen will undergo trial by ordeal. This was the King's verdict. He has hardened his heart. The Queen puts her faith in you, praying that you will come in time to rescue her."

Lancelot pulled himself upright. He leaned against the wall. "Where and when?" he asked, straining for the reply.

The messenger answered exactly as Modred had instructed; then rode back to the King's House and received his reward. Modred sent messages to Ither, Brodeshead, the Master of Alton Priors and the many other pawns in the great game, in which he would win or lose all.

"Be ready for the staghunt!" He sent the same message to the High Lord of the Saxons. Modred laughed as he watched his messengers ride out. It was an ass they were hunting, not a stag. King Arthur's love for the Queen had checked him, but only briefly: now her love for him would destroy them both. Modred considered his position with satisfaction: he had gained the King's confidence; the King trusted him above all others. Lancelot would carry off Guinevere, and that fool Arthur would be forced to battle. And when that happened, the steps to the King's Seat would rise clear before him. A few more moves in the game, just a few more, and the King would be helpless in check.

The King murmured his wife's name. He took her in his arms. He stared down into her eyes.

"Dear heart, this is no time for words," Guinevere said. She was light-hearted and content.

"I cannot allow the trial to take place," said King Arthur. "I will give up my kingdom, I will give up all I have. Let another man sit in the King's Seat. We will spend what time we have left together."

"We have one another. Seven days of happiness is a long time. And I am not afraid to die."

"You were innocent. I doubted you," the King said.

"You were possessed by your high ideals. I had to win you back to the real world." She was smiling. "You are here. I will put everything else out of my mind."

"I am thinking of the trial," said Arthur. "We cannot impose our will on God. He will not send a sign to prove He lives and reigns. You will go down to death because you are innocent."

"We have seven more days," said Guinevere. "I made my choice during the investigation. I chose between a lifetime of doubt and distrust, in which you would close yourself off from me entirely, and this one week, living as lovers, man and wife, forsaking all other. Dear heart, I chose the finest thing I could ever hope to have." She laughed. "Do not grieve. A week is a long time."

She laid her head against his shoulder. His arms were round her, holding her there. She knew that he must fulfil the task of founding his kingdom in peace; she had chosen accordingly. She looked down the coming days: a week of absolute happiness was a long time. The sun dropped below the skyline in a glow of red. The first day was over.

Soon they would part. Soon death would come

between them. Against this knowledge their love grew stronger every hour.

They climbed the watch-tower and looked out across the hills of Britain. A cool gentle stirring of air touched them as they stood on the tower roof. Small grey clouds streaked the western sky, meshing the last light of the sun.

"The world could be another Eden," Arthur said.

Guinevere said, "We have no time to waste in sorrow." She began to sing an old soldier's song which Arthur had taught her long ago:

> *"My sweetheart's mouth is paradise:*
> *There journey's end should be—*
> *No girl ever lay in Death's bone-arms—*
> *He swung his scythe at me."*

Arthur looked down at her and found himself smiling. His sadness was no match for her courage. She meant to have her few days of happiness.

A last glow of sunlight brightened the greying sky and then was gone. Dusk slid into night; the second day was over. On the third day a storm broke out, but Arthur and Guinevere hardly noticed it. They were alone together in the King's Room. There the third day slipped unnoticed into the fourth.

They sent for Guy. He meant more to them than a jester; he had become a friend. But unlike them, Guy had no great love to uphold him. In this moment of parting he did not know how to act.

"Why aren't you laughing?" asked the King, but Guy was in tears. He tried desperately to hide his weeping. He looked at the King and Queen and saw that they were in love and full of courage. In their happiness they took pains to hide their lack of hope, but this too Guy saw.

"Laugh?" He bit his lips. "I will keep my laughter till later," he said, "for he who laughs last laughs best." Then he shook his narrow little head. He could hardly have said anything more unfortunate. "Forgive me,

High King," he stammered. "I—" He was completely distraught and stumbling over his words. He tried desperately to laugh and to keep back his tears.

"Let be, Guy," said Guinevere. "We did not call you to amuse us. We wanted to thank you for your loyalty and friendship." She rose and kissed the little jester on both cheeks. His tears were like salt in her mouth. The sun went down, and the fifth day was over.

At first light on the sixth day they rode out together across the fields. The hills were blue in the cool clear light of the morning air. Everything that could be said had been said. Vehemently the King had declared that he would stand down from the King's Seat and free Guinevere from undergoing trial by ordeal. Equally vehemently she had demanded that he too make a sacrifice: to carry on his great task, to keep his country united, to maintain peace, to protect his people, he must allow the trial. "I will ride out from this House

under formal escort. I will not bid you goodbye. This whole week has been our farewell. Let our parting be as I wish it."

They rode back to the King's House and spent the last day together.

He looked down into her eyes. They were steadfast under his gaze. Everything had been arranged; everything had been said.

Time slipped past. The sun sank and the sixth day was over. They did not see it go.

When King Arthur awoke on the seventh day, having slept for a few hours only, Guinevere had gone.

Escorted by Sir Bedivere, Sir Gawain and other lords, Guinevere the Queen rode through the early morning to the place where the trial was to be held. Her hair blew back on the wind. She looked pale, but she was tranquil as a holy woman, and smiling a little. A priest rode beside her carrying a cross.

The road was lined with people: men, woman and children. "May God protect you!" many called as Guinevere rode by. Some jeered: they had condemned her even before the trial had been held or the verdict given. Some were compassionate, some curious, some hoping for excitement. But whatever the doubters said, whether they shouted or whispered, Guinevere's face did not change.

"St. John tells us that God is love," the priest said, to comfort her. "If only mortal men could fathom His ways! We must hope that He will send a sign." But he was trying to convince himself of something he did not believe.

On an impulse the priest rode up to Bedivere. He said in entreaty: "The Queen is innocent, sir!"

"I have my orders, and must carry them out," Bedivere said. His years in the King's House had taught him obedience.

They rode on across the hills. Time and again Sir Gawain had to spur his horse forward to clear a way for the Queen and her escort. The people began to run. A show like this came only once in a lifetime. They were anxious not to miss a moment of it.

The judges and the priests had made the preparations for trial by ordeal. They had roped off a part of the field to keep back the crowd. Monks and priests, striking while the iron was hot, were calling the crowds to repent. An altar had been set up. Everything was in readiness for the saying of Mass. The Bishop was kneeling in prayer.

The crowd was noisy and restless. Men and women argued endlessly whether the Queen were guilty. Quick-witted bakers had brought along trays of cakes and pasties, and a man with a dancing bear was doing well. Thus the people waited for the ordeal to begin and for God to send a sign.

"God give me strength," prayed Lancelot. He stared at Bors, who had ridden to the top of a hill overlooking the place of trial. Bors was to give the sign that would send them sweeping down from the skyline to rescue the Queen.

Lionel had drawn his sword in readiness. He gave Lancelot a searching look.

"Does it go well with you?"

Lancelot nodded, though his shirt was soaked with blood. The ride had used up a good deal of his strength and some of his wounds had re-opened. "You and Bors are to carry off the Queen, no matter how she protests."

Lionel nodded. "We will carry her safely to Brittany!"

Lancelot stared ahead. All he could do now was to wait for Bors to give the sign. Every man knew his part. He himself was too weak to undertake the long hard ride to the shore and the sea-crossing into Brittany; his friends would carry the Queen to safety beyond the sea, while he lay hidden somewhere in Britain, recovering his strength. Sir Eric de Maris had already ridden on to the sea-coast, making the preparations for a safe escape. He would stable fresh horses at stages along the way, and would gather together groups of armed men to delay possible pursuers.

Lancelot and his companions waited. Soon they must sweep down to the attack—just as the Queen and her escort dismounted. Would the people help them to snatch her away to safety? The only chance lay in bold and decisive action.

Lancelot thought of the King. He could not understand, and no longer wanted to understand, how the King could have consented to sacrifice the Queen. He had once sworn to serve the King's House. That promise drove him now to save the Queen.

He watched Bors through the trees. It could not be much longer. For a moment Lancelot closed his eyes. He felt dazed and exhausted.

"Lord God, let me fulfil this one task," he whispered. Once the Queen had been carried off to safety, he hoped to find some measure of rest in the hut that belonged to the old holy man of the woods. And then he would be strong enough to cross to his fortress in Brittany.

And what then? Perhaps he would at last be able to sleep when he was weary.

Bors flung up his arm.

"Forward!" shouted Lancelot, and set spurs to his horse.

Queen Guinevere dismounted. Every man, woman and child was gazing at her. The Bishop stepped forward and took her hand.

"She is innocent," whispered the priest who had accompanied her. He stared urgently at the Bishop. Then, ashamed, he lowered his eyes. God had founded His Church to give the people faith and strength. In this critical moment the Church must not show itself weak and unsure.

As if to comfort him, the Queen gave the Bishop a slight smile. Sir Gawain and Sir Bedivere and the other knights had also dismounted, giving their horses into the charge of servants waiting nearby.

"Lady," said the Bishop, "we will pray that God will help us all—"

A battle cry rang out on the air, swelling to a roar of voices as the whole crowd took it up. There was a thunder-burst of drumming hooves. The tumult increased; the crowd broke ranks and went stumbling back; a baker selling cakes was trampled underfoot; in an instant all was confusion and panic.

Sir Gawain drew his sword and sprang forward.

"Lancelot, the traitor!" he cried, but the priest caught his arm and held him back.

"Save the Queen!" shouted Sir Lionel.

Sir Bors drove his horse forward between the Bishop and the Queen. He seized Guinevere and hauled her up across his saddle-bow. Sir Bedivere sprang forward to seize the reins, but he stumbled. In the melée he did not realise that the priest had deliberately tripped him.

"Forgive us, oh Lord," whispered the priest, "for we none of us know what we are doing."

Sir Lionel and Lancelot galloped forward, forcing a way through the crowd. There was shouting on all sides;

struggles broke out. A group of servants flung themselves on the escorts' horses and galloped away, shouting to the peasants:

"Give them a chance to escape!"

Knights and peasants sprawled over the altar in a struggling mass. Sir Gawain was cursing. Someone seized the executioner by the slack of his tunic, lifted him, and tossed him on the fire.

The priest gazed around sadly. Had the people really hoped for a verdict from God? He saw the Bishop's bewildered face. Did he too realize that by staging the Ordeal the Church had tried to compel God to prove He lived? Ashamed, the priest lowered his eyes.

Lancelot glanced over his shoulder. No one yet in pursuit. Sir Bors and Sir Lionel galloped ahead of him; the others were following close behind. All were there excepting John and Owen who had been left behind to stir up still greater confusion and to urge the people to resist. The first two knights broke away to the right. The company was to disperse in this way, two by two, to lead the pursuers astray.

Sir Lancelot swung east. He sprawled forward on his horse's neck, one hand clinging to its mane as he rode on, hour after hour, the other pressed against the deepest wound. The country was deserted. He rode on, seeing no one, feverish and exhausted.

The afternoon was drawing towards dusk and the horse had dropped to a walk, when Lancelot reached the wood. The world had shrunk around him, dwindling until he was not even conscious of the silent trees through which the horse picked its way. A single thought possessed him: he must hang on to the horse's mane.

The horse stopped in front of a simple hut, someone caught at the reins, but Lancelot did not know it. Nor did he realize that he was carried inside and laid down on a bed. He was unconscious.

133

15

Modred, Content

In the King's Room that lay behind the Great Hall, the King was pacing restlessly, full of despair. For the sake of the kingdom he had allowed Guinevere to suffer trial by ordeal. Now he asked himself how he could possibly have allowed her to go.

Gawain flung the door open and strode into the room, with Bedivere and a priest at his heels. He could hardly speak coherently.

"High King—my lord King—the Queen—the Queen has been carried off, the traitor Lancelot has snatched away the Queen—!"

Here at the latest possible moment, was the miracle the King had longed for. A rush of relief filled him. Guinevere was safe.

Gawain described what had happened. He told the King how Lancelot and his friends had come storming downhill, and how in the tumult and melée it had been impossible to pursue them.

"And the escort?" asked the King. "Why did none of them ride in pursuit?" He forced himself to be practical, but his heart was shouting with joy.

"Our horses were seized, High King," said Bedivere. He explained how servants had ridden the horses away.

"Who gave the order? Has it been investigated?"

Bedivere nodded. "It was Sir Modred, High King. It seems he instructed the servants to support any attempt to carry off his sister the Queen."

The finest of my knights, thought Arthur. He had done the King true service—he alone among them all.

"Shall I take a troop of horsemen and pursue them? Lancelot will make for Brittany." Sir Gawain gave the King a searching look.

"Give me time to think and to recover myself," said King Arthur. And Gawain, Bedivere and the priest withdrew.

While Lancelot lay in a high fever, slowly winning back his strength, Sir Bors and Guinevere set sail for Brittany.

Sir Modred was filled with content and satisfaction. It had been brilliant of him to warn Lancelot, and to work the servants into the plans for the Queen's rescue. That move above all others had assured him of the King's friendship and absolute trust. And Guinevere and Lancelot also owed him gratitude—or thought they did so.

Days went by. But there was still no word of Lancelot. Men said that he had carried the Queen to Brittany, which was unshakeably loyal to him. The King's knights demanded vengeance. Gawain's allies were set on marching against Lancelot, and demanded that the King should muster the army.

In this mighty game of winner-takes-all, Modred now held a position that was practically unassailable. He was triumphant and certain of victory.

Arthur considered for a long time before he did indeed muster the army. Some of the younger lords had already ridden away to join Lancelot. Such splitting and argument might well lead to civil war. It was essential to act quickly and decisively to put an end to doubt and uncertainty.

The King sent out criers to every corner of the kingdom calling his lords and his men to arms. Some came from the greatest strongholds, others from poor

steadings, to gather together under King Arthur's stand-
ard, each bringing his own armed men eager for the
fight. Sir Cynric came, but not the mighty Ither. Old
Pellinore came, but the Lord of Brodeshead stayed away.
Kay came, but the Master of Alton Priors did not.
Although many came, others held back, waiting for
Modred's message, ready to hunt down the stag.

As was his custom, King Arthur rode out each day
to the camp beyond the walls of the King's House. More
men came every hour. He spoke with them all, no matter
what their rank. The soldiers sat at the camp-fires and
urged one another on until their blood was up and they
were fighting mad. This campaign against Brittany
promised to be a mighty enterprise.

The King saw the bright tents and the gay banners;
he spoke with a throng of old friends; he was deeply
touched by their loyalty; but his heart was dry, and his
anxious thoughts grieved over his kingdom.

The army stood ready. It was not yet at full strength,
but strong enough to march against Brittany in good
hope of success.

King Arthur called his knights and commanders
together, and in their presence, named Modred to sit
in the King's Seat for the duration of the campaign, and
gave the kingdom into his charge. In great humility
Modred pledged himself to accept the task.

"No man can step into your shoes, High King. I can
only try to carry out this charge as best I may."

The army broke camp, formed ranks, and marched
for the sea. Modred stood on the walls of the King's
House and watched the horsemen riding out and the
foot-soldiers marching to war. What were they but small,
trivial pawns in his great game?

Abruptly Modred knew that he was being closely
watched. He looked around him: at the army, at the

16

For He Was King

Queen Guinevere sat in a small room in Lancelot's
fortress, alone with her thoughts. She tried to review all
that had happened in the past few months. It seemed
very complex, very confused. How difficult it was to
understand what drove men in their search for fame,
power, honour; how difficult to guess what or who it
was that had shattered the peace of the King's House.

She heard footsteps in the passage. The door opened
and a man came in. He was wearing the grey hessian
tunic of the poor. As she watched, he stumbled and
reached out to the wall for support.

Guinevere was caught unawares by a surge of astonishment and grief. Was this Lancelot? She saw a face
drained of colour, hollowed and worn with fatigue.
The man's mouth was drawn with pain. A skeletal
stooping man in a rough grey tunic—

"Oh Lancelot," she whispered.

He raised his head and looked at her. He had longed
for her through loneliness and in high fever, but never
as greatly as he did at this moment. In desperation he
tried to speak in sober and practical terms.

He told her what had happened since the night he
had come to her room, accounting to her—and to
himself—for what he had done. "We must go together
to the King. Together we can convince him that we are
innocent."

Guinevere shook her head. "You are not yet strong

enough, Sir Lancelot. Let me go alone. I will tell the King the truth. He will not doubt my word. It is not yet too late, but time is running out fast."

Lancelot bowed. Perhaps this was the better way. He had done all he could. Guinevere had called him "Sir Lancelot". She wanted to set a distance between them.

"Ride to the King then, since you wish it so. Tell him that I have never broken faith. Speak for me, my lady the Queen, stand as my advocate. You know why I acted as I did. Tell the King that I will come to him as soon as I have strength enough for the journey."

Queen Guinevere rose. "You are the King's true man, and have defended his honour, and mine, and the kingdom's. I thank you for it, and for your friendship, and for your loyalty."

Lancelot had risen as she rose, though he had to grip the table for support. His eyes were full of tears, but he kept a look of bravery in his face.

"We all rode out for the King's honour, and for the kingdom," he said quietly. "But when the time of testing came, we rode on, past one another, like people lost in the night. Go to King Arthur and tell him that I acted as best I could, given what I am, but that above and beyond this, I have never broken faith with him."

A few hours later, Guinevere rode out across the Breton hills with Eric de Maris at her side. Her heart was full of happiness; in a few days she would see the King. God had given her this extra gift. In that last week with the King she had surrendered her life and her love. Now, her heart filled with gratitude and hope, she rode out to see the King once more, journeying towards the place where his army lay encamped.

King Arthur sat in his tent, with his commanders gathered round him. The discussions were all over. The army, which had landed in Brittany only a few hours earlier, stood ready to march.

The King gave one last order: "Be sure there is no looting, nor, wherever possible, unnecessary killing. We are not fighting an enemy: we are marching to regain old friends." The unity of the kingdom was of over-riding importance.

In the camp the soldiers were singing:

"My sweetheart's mouth is paradise:
There journey's end should be—"

Guinevere, the King thought: journey's end. Soon he would take her in his arms again. God in His mercy had given him this extra gift.

King Arthur rose. He had meant to dismiss the commanders, but at that moment the tent flap was pulled aside. Sir Bedivere strode in, blazing with anger. "High King, my lord King—" he began, "High King, Modred has made himself master of the kingdom. He has sent out criers proclaiming himself King of Britain, and has mustered a mighty army!"

For a moment the tent was still as death. The news was toweringly strange; so unbelievable that the King's commanders could not grasp it. Then a clamour of voices burst out.

The truth broke upon the King with agonizing clearness. He saw exactly what had happened. It lay before him: the real and terrible truth, every detail of it. Modred had sent Lancelot to Guinevere's room that night. Modred had sown doubt and suspicion. Modred had driven home the wedge that had split the King's household apart.

King Arthur was conscious of the mounting anger of the men around him, but he did not hear their cries and exclamations. He raised his hand and looked at Bedivere. He was the King; they must see that he held command.

"What manner of army has Modred mustered?"

"The Saxons have sent an army of invasion to his aid. Ither, Brodeshead and many other men have ranged themselves under his banner!"

141

I must choose now, thought Arthur. He was conscious of a sudden great weariness. He thought of Guinevere. A few days, a few hours, were all that lay between them, yet that might be too long. He must choose between his own happiness and the good of his kingdom.

The commanders were watching him: for he was the King. Every hour was now of vital importance—a hundred times more important than before word came of Modred's breaking of faith. Each day that passed gave Modred a better chance of making himself impregnable. The King knew that he must set aside his weariness. He must close his mind to his longing for Guinevere. He could still hear the soldiers singing a long way off. Their voices were blurred and distant.

The King gave his orders.

"Call the men to arms. Get them on board ship with all possible dispatch. Set sail for Britain. Modred is waiting there!" He looked round the circle. "Sir Cynric, I lay another task on you. Ride to Lancelot. Tell him that I know he is my true man. Tell him that as the darkness falls over us we count on him to stand at our side. Ask him to cross to Britain and to range himself with me and with his hearth-companions."

Sir Cynric bowed. The King went on:

"Escort the Queen to the Convent of Medeshamstead. Tell her that I will come to her there!" King Arthur glanced round at his men. He heard Merlin's voice speak down the years: "Your happiness runs high, but it cannot do so for ever."

The King looked at his commanders. "It will be a mighty battle," he said. "Make ready. The stake is all or nothing."

His hand gripped the table-board for support, but he held himself erect. For he was the King.

142

17

The Battle

In the early dawn the two hosts were drawn up for battle. On the one side the light-bringers, on the other the men of the dark.

That night King Arthur had lain restless in his tent. Only a few more hours, and the battle against Modred would begin. He groaned in his sleep, for he was dreaming.

A serpent was sliding through the grass. He saw it creep towards him, but he could stir neither foot nor finger; only his eyes moved, looking desperately round for help. The countryside lay deserted. It was moonset, and far in the distance river-water glinted in the last of the light. Was that Merlin—? "Merlin, Merlin!" the King cried in his dream, and his old tutor came closer, with a grave sad smile in his face, and pointed to the water.

"Every river at last makes its way to the open sea. Journey's end."

The serpent slid nearer. Abruptly Merlin was gone. Welwyn came riding across the fields, and the King, trapped in his dream, called to him for help.

"That serpent, High King?" Welwyn reined in his horse. "I would help you gladly, but no man can defeat the dragon that lies in another's heart." Welwyn rode on, and the serpent slid closer. Its coils looked thicker now, and still more manifold. Its tongue flickered; venom burned the living grass.

Modred sprang up beside the serpent. His laughter

143

rang out in the night. King Arthur looked desperately around him. Could no one help? Was that little Guy approaching? "A man must go out into the dark to see the stars, High King!" called Guy. The night-sky cleared: and as Guy pointed, the King saw light through the clouds. The serpent slid closer still, and King Arthur saw the flickering tongue dart out, saw the head rear to strike—

"High King, my lord King, wake up!"

King Arthur woke with a start, to find himself cold and sweating. He stared round in bewilderment. Guy was standing at his bedside looking down at him.

"I was dreaming," said the King, as he came to himself.

"I heard you call in your sleep," said Guy.

"I was lying in the grass—there was a serpent—it came creeping towards me," said Arthur. He related his dream.

Guy gave the King a searching look. Surely this dream reflected the image of a man caught in the coils of endless difficulties—Did the King himself, finest and most knightly of men, fear his own weakness? Was he grieving over a sense of guilt? Or did his dreams foreshadow the conflict to come?

A glow of light crept over the skyline: dayspring, and the first stirring in the camp, soon growing louder as the army set weapons and gear in readiness for the coming battle.

"High King," said Guy, "perhaps this dream is a sign. Try to come to terms with Modred. Try to gain time until Lancelot can bring his men to stand at your side."

King Arthur looked at the little jester and smiled.

The day promised to be hot. The hills of Britain lay green and gentle in the sunlight of early morning.

In a dark cloak over a dark mail shirt, with a black helmet on his head, Modred sat his horse at the head of his troops. His commanders were at his side. He looked

out across the valley. On the hills opposite, Arthur's army was drawn up for battle.

"We will soon see what it is that makes a man," Lord Ither said, laughing. "Perhaps in this battle he may stand to fight at last. I waited for him once before—you recall our plan, Modred?—but another came before him, a proper man—That was a fight to remember! While Arthur dallies, talking, other men ride out to fight. Give the signal to attack, High King, and let us show that strength and courage mean more in the making of a man than any milky talk!"

"We are fighting for a third part of the spoils, as you have promised, Lord Modred," said the Saxon leader. "Give the signal to attack, my lord. For a third part of the spoils I would ride to the further side of Hell!"

Modred nodded. He was about to draw his sword and give the signal; but Ither checked him. "See, a rider—" He pointed across the valley.

"Arthur sends us an envoy," said the Saxon chief.

Sir Bedivere came riding up at the gallop.

"Give the signal to attack, High King!" Ither said impatiently. "The time for words—for idle, meaningless talk—that time is past!"

K.A.—K 145

Modred laughed. "Don't steal a single moment of my triumph," he said. "A cat plays with a mouse before devouring it."

"True enough. I will relish your game with Arthur," said Ither.

Sir Bedivere reined in, facing Modred.

"I come in the name of Arthur the King. He asks for a parley, not out of fear or from lack of courage, but out of compassion, for if this battle is joined friend will fight against friend, Briton against Briton, and the kingdom will be shattered. For this reason, and this only, the King offers to negotiate."

Modred nodded. His face was grave. "I am willing," he said. "Let the King ride down into the valley, bringing no more than twelve horsemen with him. I will ride down to meet him with no more than twelve horsemen of my own—on condition that no weapon shall be drawn!"

"Let it be so," said Sir Bedivere, and turned his horse.

Ither spat on the ground. "I am sick of talk, High King," he said angrily. "Give the signal to attack, and let us ride down to live or die on the battlefield."

Modred laughed. "I want to see Arthur once more." He spoke softly, but as he went on, his voice grew stronger. "I want to see him kick in the coils. I want to watch him as he sees that nothing is left of all his fine ideals. Year after year I have had to listen to his high-sounding words, year after year I have had to hear men praise him. His care for the kingdom—his Round Table —seeking the Grail—a bringer of light—and now all this comes to nothing. Justice, truth, mercy, understanding of one's fellow men, these things are not the making of a man. I want to see him kick in the coils, do you hear me, I want to see him writhe!" Modred was almost shouting. For a moment even Lord Ither was taken aback by this furious outburst.

But Modred quickly regained his self-control. "Let me

146

have my moment of triumph, Lord Ither," he said, more calmly.

"I will ride down into the valley with you," Ither said.

They faced each other: King Arthur with twelve of the Knights of the Round Table, and Modred with twelve of his chiefs.

Sir Gawain was watching the King. What did he hope to gain? "Do not trust Modred," Sir Pellinore had said. The old fighter stood beside Arthur. His hand lay, apparently casual, on the hilt of his sword. but his muscles were tensed; he stood ready to strike.

"I do not trust Modred," the King had replied. "I am only hoping for a miracle—" He had given his men instructions to strike at once if Modred or one of his fellows drew a sword. So they faced each other: full of distrust and hatred. Modred laughed and said: "Out with your propositions, Arthur; time is pressing. Come, your hands are empty, you have nothing to offer. You're a fool, Arthur. All your life long you have held by your false image of humanity, and gone on reaching out for what you could never have—and now you face me with empty hands. What sort of proposals did you hope to put to me? Go away, go back to Guinevere and leave the kingdom to me. There is no room here for a fool like you!"

King Arthur looked at his wife's brother. Was there anything left in this man to which he might yet appeal, to save from destruction all he had spent his life in building?

Their eyes met. The instant stretched out to eternity. And then, abruptly, Arthur saw an adder in the grass in front of Modred. The snake came sliding slowly forward. Had the adder found its master?

My dream, thought Arthur. He heard Modred laugh. The voice came from a great distance.

"Come, Arthur, you fool. Where are all your fine, empty words? Usually you're cram-full of them. Are you hoping to appeal to my better nature? To my sense of justice, perhaps? Are you going to plead for the unity of the kingdom? Speak out, Arthur!"

The adder came coiling and sliding through the grass. King Arthur saw the flickering tongue, the small fierce eyes. I have used up all my words, he thought. The snake hissed and reared to strike. Had no one else seen it?

"I am waiting, Arthur." Modred's voice came from a long way off. "I am waiting, dumbskull."

At that moment Ither saw the adder. He drew his sword, forgetting the terms on which they met, and swung it up to cut off the creature's head. The steel flashed in the air.

"Treason!" Gawain leaped forward. In an instant Pellinore, Bedivere, Modred, the Saxon chief—all had drawn their swords.

"Stop, stop!" cried King Arthur. But it was too late.

"To arms! Forward for King Arthur and for Britain!" cried Pellinore.

"Forward for Modred!" shouted Lord Ither. The two armies, drawn up on the hills and facing one another across the valley, stirred and began to advance.

Appalled, Arthur stared around him. Could he still prevent battle being joined?

"Show us what makes a man, Arthur!" Ither strode towards him: a mighty and threatening figure. "If you are a man, show us—stand and fight!"

King Arthur drew Excalibur from its scabbard. The world faded round him: nothing was left but the need to fight. He brought his sword slashing mightily down, blow after blow, and Ither, who had once called himself "the Terrible", was driven back. Modred saw it and ran to his aid. "Stand fast, Ither!"

But Ither could not stand his ground. He saw now what it was that made a man and he fell back, ducking and dodging to avoid Arthur's blows. His shield splintered, his hauberk was ripped apart. "Have mercy!"

he cried, but Arthur's sword came down on him. Ither the Terrible fell, crying out. His blood stained the grass.

The two armies fell upon one another, lusting for the kill. Saxes, cudgels, swords came crashing down on mail and shield. Dust came smoking up from the battlefield. Men were mown down like grass under the scythe. A rain of sweat and blood. But the dust would not settle.

Little Guy had been swept along in the fury of the first storming attack. He had snatched up a fallen sax to fight for King Arthur and for Britain. In earlier days he had made the King laugh, and lightened the King's solitude. Now he gave the King the dearest thing he had: Guy gave his life.

Swinging the sax, he forced his way forward, a small slight figure dodging between the shields and under the lances. Directly ahead he saw Excalibur flash in the sunlight. He fought his way forward; God saw him safe to his place at the King's side.

"My lord King!" he cried. Arthur the King glimpsed his jester's face. It was bright and ardent. Then a Saxon chief flung his lance. It glanced off a swinging shield and struck Guy: the mighty shaft striking deep past the small breast-bone, through the narrow ribs.

"Guy! Guy!"

Sir Gawain, Sir Kay and Sir Pellinore sprang forward to fill the breach as the King dropped to his knees by his jester. The battle raged round them: the screams of horses, the cries of the wounded and the dying. Knights of the Round Table stood shoulder to shoulder, forming a wall that ringed round the King and Guy, to pay the fighting man's last honours to the jester. "Guy—" the King said again, gazing down at the thin face that was stained with blood.

"A man must go out into the dark if he hopes to see the stars, High King," said Guy. The earlier years went toppling past him. "Do you remember—I said Death must have his harvest. It seems he heard me."

"Guy!" The blood on the King's face was tracked with tears. "Hold fast!"

Guy shook his head. "A wise man goes consenting to his death, High King. The world is crying out for the fruits of the earth, it's not so bad a thing to be worm's meat."

He tried to sit up, struggling for strength enough to speak a last word. The King bent over him.

"My lord the High King," whispered Guy, "forward for King Arthur and for Britain." He fell back. The light faded from his eyes.

King Arthur closed the staring eyes and laid him down, then seized his sword and went storming forward, blind with fury, straight for the man who had killed little Guy. He flung himself at his adversary. Excalibur flashed down to the kill.

There was blood and still more blood. Sweat, and still more sweat. Dust, and still more dust. Friend and foe clashed bloodily, each resolute to stand his ground. They struggled for a footing on the bodies of the wounded, they stumbled on the bodies of the dead. There lay a dying horse, there a wounded man moaned for water, there a broken voice choked on a cry of fear. Saxes, arrows, lances flashed home, sinking into throat, stomach, and heart.

The Knights of the Round Table fought with mighty courage. No man offered mercy. They had forgotten their Order's ideals. For even ideals went down before the swords.

The earth was steeped in blood. Wounded men lay there, crying for mercy: but the chieftains drove their horses forward over the dying men, for mercy too, went down to sax and sword. "God, God, oh God!" Sir Pellinore cried out in grief as he saw the terror round him. A stray arrow drove deep into his skull, piercing the eye-socket. Sir Pellinore crashed to the ground. For knights and the knightly code went down to spear and arrow-shaft.

King Arthur laid about him, striking out like a stag bayed by the hunt. He had lost his leg-guards and the sleeves of his hauberk had been torn away, but his helmet and his mail still glinted bright as gold in the bravery of knightly gear, and his sword came flashing down. But his face was no longer ardent and kingly. For kingship too went down with the dying men.

The lances cut through living flesh. Arrows drove down thick as rain, bristling in back and shoulder, piercing through a man's chest to the lungs. The sun went down that day in a glow of blood; and light, too, went down into the dark that day, and died with the dead in that battle.

The green earth was wrapped in blood and dust like a dead man in his winding sheet.

King Arthur stared around him, dazed and bewildered. Where were his friends? And where was the enemy? Was there no one left?

There were no friends now, and no foes. Friend and foe had gone down together into the dark.

Struggling for breath, the King leaned on his sword. He came slowly to himself. The battlefield stretched out around him. Here and there a cry, the last breath rattling in the throat, a whispered word. The grass had been fresh and green and springing in the clear light of early morning; now it was strewn with the dead, with bloody arms, with trampled men and horses. A little way off he thought he saw the glint of lake-water. Was there water enough in all the world to wash the green grass clean again?

King Arthur stared around him. His heart was heavy and cold. Where were the men who had been his friends, his counsellors, his hearth-companions? Tears for this suffering, this total destruction, this godforsaken loneliness, ran down his face.

"High King—!" It was Bedivere's voice.

"Bedivere, where are the others?" King Arthur caught him by the shoulders.

"They have all gone down in the battle."

For a moment King Arthur stared at Bedivere, horrified, uncomprehending. Then he looked out again across the battlefield. Bedivere grasped his shoulder in a rush of panic. "High King, over there—" His face was the colour of ash as he pointed far across the field.

King Arthur held his breath as he saw a solitary figure rise up among the dead. Was it Death himself? It was laughing in the dusk like the Lord of Hell reviewing the armies of his kingdom.

"Modred!" whispered Bedivere, appalled.

Modred stood out against the darkening sky. He was armed and clad in some dark sombre colour. His head was black, and he wore no helmet. His laughter rang clear across the valley.

Then King Arthur ran at him, sword in hand. The sky cleared and the moon sailed free of the clouds. The King's armour was blanched and fired by moonshine. Modred saw him coming, laughed, and stooped to seize a fallen spear.

The King raised his sword as if to crush some creeping venomous thing. Bedivere saw Excalibur flash down. A terrible cry rang through the air. Modred crashed forward, but as he fell, the spear came flying from his hand. It struck the King. For a moment King Arthur stood, leaning heavily on his sword, and looked down at the defeated Modred. Then he sank slowly to his knees and toppled forward.

Bedivere stood as if nailed fast to the ground. He saw the King sink and fall. Then he ran towards him. "High King, my lord High King!" His hands felt stiff and useless. He fumbled to unfasten Arthur's torn and dented mail. He tried to staunch the wound. Bending down, he listened for the beat of the King's heart. The King still lived; he had not yet gone forward into death.

It was a long time before King Arthur opened his eyes. "I am a dead man, Bedivere."

"Let me go for help, High King."

With difficulty, King Arthur shook his head. "It is over, Bedivere. No mourning—Death too must have his harvest." Inch by inch the King stretched out his hand to touch his sword. "Bedivere, take my sword and throw it far into the lake."

Since he entered the King's House years before, Sir Bedivere had lived a life of strict obedience: he nodded and stood up. He took the sword and made his way across the field of the dead. The silence was that of another world. He came to the lake-shore. And there he stood.

Excalibur lay shining in his hands. Must he surrender this glorious sword, unconquered and unconquerable from the day of its making, to the cold dark water? The sword that lay in his hands was like a live thing, still, but with its own bright strength.

On impulse he thrust the famous sword under a bush and went quickly back to the King. He knelt down. The King still lived.

"High King," began Bedivere, "let me—"

The King's eyes looked at him. Bedivere fell silent.

"Throw the sword into the water," whispered King Arthur. "This is my last order, my last wish on this earth."

In shame, Bedivere rose and went back to the lake-shore. Again, he stood there, hesitating. Excalibur lay in his hands. This sword was a tangible symbol of the King's great enterprise. Should it not be kept safe as proof and promise of what had been and what might be again—the sword of Arthur, the once and future king?

Holding the sword in both hands Sir Bedivere went back once more to the King.

"High King—"

But the King looked at him, and Bedivere was profoundly ashamed.

"Has your obedience too gone down before the spears? Bedivere, if a man lives by the sword, by the sword he shall die. You think of Excalibur as a symbol of my kingship, but you are wrong; the true symbol is the act of throwing Excalibur into the lake."

And so Sir Bedivere made his way through the silent dead for the third time and came to the lake-shore, and there he carried out King Arthur's final wish on earth; he threw the sword far out into the cold dark water.

King Arthur lay alone in the moonlit night. His life lay far behind him, and with it all the cares of his kingship. He looked up to the kingdom of God.

Sword had gone down to sword, sax to sax, spear to spear; those who believed in the force of arms lay dead: the force of arms had killed them. The struggling, the bright hopes, the uncertainties all lay behind him. The King smiled. He had hoped to be a light-bringer in a dark age. Only now, as his life came to its close, did he see light spring out: the brilliance of the stars: the opening of the doors of God. He saw the darkness lifting and the starlight streaming down to fuse into a single brightness; higher and higher rose the steeps of light. The firmament stretched out, infinite reaching into infinity, eternal reaching into eternity. How long was the way to the doors of God?

The judgment had been made, the questions answered. King Arthur's eyes closed. He had gone past their seeing, up the steeps of light. His face was tranquil. When Sir Bedivere returned he found King Arthur dead.

18

Merlin

Merlin searched, grieving, for words to bring his chronicle to a fitting close as he sat there, at the rough-hewn board.

With the death of King Arthur, Britain went down again into the dark. Once more the lords made war on one another, fighting over hunting-rights, fishing-rights, women and land, and once more Saxons, Scots and Picts came storming on their raids.

Britain was a place of endless weeping. All across the land were burnt-out steadings, captured strongholds, plundered churches. The shining and glory of the past lay hidden under the ash and rubble of a new age.

Merlin looked out through his window at the wide grey sky. What else? What were the last words of all? Arthur had brought light into Britain. What had happened to the principles of justice he had established? What remained of all he had built? The code of knighthood had gone down with his knights into the dust of the battlefield.

The great Halls and strongholds that the knights had raised were toppled now into darkness. The churches and the convents were empty echoing places, harbouring none but ghosts.

What were the last words of all?

Should he describe how Queen Guinevere had died in a convent, soon after Arthur's death? Should he set down that Lancelot had laid her beside Arthur in a narrow grave?

156

I have carried out the task I set myself, thought Merlin. The light that Arthur kindled shone out in the darkness of his time; it is scattered but not extinguished; the sparks fly yet.

What were the last words of all?

Men are fools. Such wisdom as they have is a flickering dip in a great and gusty darkness. They are blind to the miracle of life. And that is why I have here set down all the strivings of King Arthur, the first truly Christian ruler of Britain.

Arthur made his journey through the dark places of life and came out into the light. In the last week of their life together he and his Queen shared the love which endures all things. Men who came after them can reach out as they did to the doors of God, while living yet their full and real lives on earth. This is the faith Arthur defended, the hope he lived by. He was a man like other men, stumbling, faulty, limited; yet this is the light he lit for those who came after him.

Merlin rose and tied together the heap of parchment. He drew his pilgrim's cloak around him, took the book under his arm and went slowly out.

A strong wind was driving the clouds across the sky. The trees were swaying, and leaves came dropping through the dusk.

Merlin walked across the hills. He passed the ruined strongholds, the burnt-out steadings, the blackened stains that marked the holocaust of a world's hope.

He was an old man, tired and solitary.

He had walked for several days before, long after moonset, he knocked at a monastery door. He asked to see the abbot.

"These are the chronicles of Arthur the King," he said quietly. He laid them on the table. "Guard them well, for if they are lost the men who come after us will trim and twist the truth."

The abbot nodded, but said nothing.

"Keep it safe for those who are not yet born, or they will deck him in their own dreams, their minds will mirror a false image; they will not see his reign as it was: a fine and shining enterprise, a reaching out to God."

Again the abbot nodded. He looked at Merlin's tired worn face; he felt the lifetime's power that lay in him. The abbot asked no questions.

That same night Merlin left the monastery. He walked out through the lonely night to meet the time of his death.

19

The History of King Arthur

What is a man's lifetime when seen against eternity?
A small and restless aching, like a nagging tooth? A
thing that begins and ends?

Year after year slipped past. In the distant monastery,
where Merlin had paused on the last day of his life, the
abbot died and was buried, and a new one chosen, and
he in his turn ruled over the abbey, and died and was
put in his grave; and after him another, and another,
and another, until one day an abbot chanced to leaf
through the old yellowed pages, on which was written
the story of King Arthur's times.

"This is a fine tale," he said a few days later to a
wandering singer, who had asked for shelter. "You
should make a song of it and sing it at hearth and hall."

The singer read the old yellowed parchments. He
made a song that told of King Arthur and the Knights of
the Round Table. But the singer did not think Merlin's
tale was fine enough. Lancelot's knightly selflessness was
past his fathoming; instead he showed him as a warrior
who slew dragons and fought against magic-makers—
the small dark people who dwell in the hollow hills. A
singer depends on applause, and a tale of steadfast
loyalty will not win many hearers.

So the singer walked the world with his new song. He
sang about great castles, beautiful damsels, enchanted
woods. Wherever he sang men praised him. His song
brought him fame and honour, and many other singers

caught it up and made their own songs of King Arthur and the Knights of the Round Table until the tales they sung were known clear across Europe and out beyond the seas. A thousand years after his death his name was a legend, and the tales that clustered about it were more widely read, more often told, more often sung, than any others. As the years went on, his true image blurred and faded into the shadows of time past.

Had he ever lived? Had his kingdom ever stood? His name hardly occurred in the oldest chronicles of all.

Yet Merlin had been right. Arthur the King was a light-bringer, and his beacon shone still, all down the years. Men turned again and again to the great story: with words and with paint, in music and in stone, they made their own images of Arthur and his knights. They began doing it on the day of his death. They are doing it still.